COWBOY INTRIGUE

BARB HAN

TORJAKE PUBLISHING

Editing: Ali Williams

Cover Design: Jacob's Cover Designs

To my family for unwavering love and support. I can't imagine doing life with anyone else. I love you guys with all my heart.

1

The frigid blast of cold air blew across Mika Taylor's face as she rolled down her truck's window, a warning of what was to come. A shiver rocked her body. A cold snap was headed to Cattle Cove and she hoped to be finished with her next case and headed somewhere warm before the winds picked up. A thin layer of cotton was the only thing keeping her bare-naked skin from exposure. Her jacket, last she remembered, was still draped across the back of the chair in her living room next to the door. Not exactly within reach now that she was more than an hour from home, parked in front of a trailer. Being forgetful was starting to become the rule, not the exception. She cursed her bad memory—a memory that was showing stress cracks now that her mother had moved in full time.

Ever since her mother's diagnosis and her father's disappearing act, concentrating was getting more and more difficult. Mika bit back a yawn. So was a good night's sleep. And just to prove Murphy's Law that everything that could go wrong would, two of her recent cases had resulted in her being threatened. In the O'Rourke case, she'd busted up a dogfighting ring with ties to a notorious crime group known for weapons smuggling. And then she'd seized a pair of Doberman Pincers from a baseball player, Andre Jimenez, who'd been recently kicked out of the league for all manner of violations, including beating his wife. The story had gone public and blown up in a big way on social media. He'd threatened Mika when she was the one taking his animals away, after a neighbor videoed him 'disciplining' them using his belt.

In her line of work, threats weren't exactly unusual. These two, for some reason, stuck with her and made her uneasy.

A break from work was coming, though. All she could think about was getting through this shift. With her mom safely in Colorado for a week visiting family, Mika would finally be able to take a hot bath after work and then curl up in bed. She had three days to sleep in and be lazy after too much overtime, along with the stress of her mother's illness. Her dad had bolted, saying he wanted to enjoy his life not be strapped with caring for his wife in the few precious years he had left. Few? Mika rolled her eyes. He was in his sixties, not nineties. The real truth was that he'd been having an affair with his administrative assistant. *Someone who cared about his needs*, he'd said. What a jerk.

It was selfish to feel lonely, but her mother moving in had killed what little social life Mika had been clinging to, and the road ahead was going to be a difficult one.

With a whole lot of effort, Mika set those thoughts aside. After this shift, she would get a break. Three whole days off. Nights too. Basically a chance to catch her breath and ready herself for the long, uphill climb that was coming with her mother's health.

Mika let out the breath she'd been holding; just thinking

about her family situation and how much it had changed on a dime was enough to make her tense up. Rather than go down that road again—the one that had her wondering how she was going to provide for her mother's care, as well as maintain some kind of life now that their circumstances had changed—she refocused on the case. Besides, she could set aside her stresses for the next week while her mother was away. There were so many good shows to binge watch, not to mention the stack of books on her nightstand she'd picked up but hadn't had time to read.

Mika gripped the handle and threw her shoulder into the door. It opened. Her sunglasses fell out of her front pocket and tumbled onto the dirt and rocks. She reached down to pick them up and bumped her head on the door as she pulled up to sitting. *Well, graceful, that was going to leave a bump.*

A deep breath and quick check in the mirror later, and she was ready to exit the county-issued vehicle. Stepping outside and into the cool morning air shouldn't send an icy chill racing down her back. She glanced around as the feeling of eyes on her caused the hair on the back of her neck to prick. Her recent transfer, so she'd be closer to home, left her in the dark about her new territory, which was a shame. And it had the tendency to make her a little more jumpy than usual.

The gate to the property was open enough to walk through, but the opening wasn't big enough for her department-issue vehicle. There were two other trailers within view. Each with a yard.

The residence she was checking on had a large dog chained to a tree in the front yard. It was her job to place a notification on the door for the owners and then if the situation wasn't corrected, seize the animal. Mika scanned the area, not wanting to be surprised by an attack. She didn't rush to the front door anymore. Not after a case where a Doberman had been left to roam in a yard with a gate half opened. She'd been tricked into thinking the dog had run away. In reality, an electric fence kept the dog inside the yard. She'd mistakenly believed he was either gone or inside the residence right up until the moment she crossed the threshold. Lucky for her, he came at her so hard she bounced out of the yard and a line he couldn't cross. He'd gone straight for her nose. She still had a tiny scar on the left side where one of his teeth cut through her skin. She'd had a nice butterfly stitch to tape the small hole closed, and a permanent reminder not to enter anyone's front lawn without the expectation a dog could come out of nowhere and attack. It had been a rookie mistake. One, she wouldn't make again.

So she surveyed this yard again carefully. There were several mesquite trees and a few oaks dotting the landscape. The trailer was old and looked like something she'd see in a meth bust on TV. White and aqua blue seemed to be the color scheme. Cinder blocks were stacked one on top of the other to form the stairs to what looked to be the front door to the single wide. Even from twenty feet out, she could see the piece of paper taped to the window. An officer had been here yesterday, and it didn't appear like the resident had been here since.

A rusted metal trash can was pushed up next to the place; it looked like the one most people used to burn trash in. The clink of heavy chains drew her gaze to a tree ten feet in front of the door. A large, dark figure loomed. She heard a low, throaty growl.

"You're okay," she said as calmly as she could. She would need her metal loop to wrangle this guy at a safe distance.

Straining to get a better look, she said a few more words meant to convey a sense of calm to the animal.

Footsteps on crunchy gravel caused her to turn toward the sound.

"Why didn't you take this poor poor dog the last time you were here?" A woman who looked to be a few years older than Mika was crossing the road. She chalked the eerie feeling of being watched that she'd had earlier to the woman heading toward Mika. The neighbor was most likely watching her through a window.

"I have to follow protocol, ma'am," Mika responded.

The woman glanced around nervously and issued a disapproving sigh.

"Are you Mrs. Lynn?" Mika asked.

"Yes. That's me. I'm Jayne Lynn." She had on pajamas, a short robe, and fuzzy house slippers. Her hands gripped the front of the robe like she was hanging on for dear life. "I'm the one who made the call because I haven't seen his truck around lately and this poor dog is always outside. I could have sworn it was crying the other night."

"How well do you know your neighbor, ma'am?" Mika asked, hoping she could get a little intel from the neighbor.

"Not at all. I've only ever seen one person and he sticks to himself. I couldn't pick him out of a lineup if my life depended on it." She sniffed and pulled a tissue out of her pocket, dabbing it under her eyes. "What kind of person leaves an animal all alone for days on end?"

Not one Mika wanted to get to know on a personal level. She shook her head in solidarity. The neighbor was good enough to make the call and file the complaint, so Mika figured Mrs. Lynn had a little bit of scoop as to what went on around her. "How long has this person lived here?"

"A couple of months," she said.

"Any idea if the person owns or rents?" Mika might be able to track down a renter. She didn't see any bowls for food or water around. This was at the very least a criminal neglect case. It was looking like animal cruelty could be added to the list. Leaving a dog to be exposed to outside elements with a thick chain around its neck, no food or water absolutely ticked the cruelty box. As much as Texas believed in individual rights, and they were strongly acknowledged, animal abuse wouldn't be tolerated.

"He rents. We all do. Elias Hunt owns everything in this area. The land has been in his family for generations. There's no way he'd sell. So, whoever lives here has to be a renter."

"And how long since you believe the person in question has been home?" Mika asked, hoping to get a timeline.

"A week at least."

"Is it possible the person works odd hours or is away on business and has someone checking on the animal?" Mika had to cover as many bases as possible while building a case.

Mrs. Lynn blew out a breath and tightened her grip on the robe. "I seriously doubt it. There'd be water somewhere and I don't ever see any. My husband says he sometimes hears a vehicle in the middle of the night when he gets up to pee."

Didn't exactly rule out the chance she was mistaken.

"And, pardon my saying so," she flashed her eyes at Mika before looking around like she half expected him to jump out from behind a bush any second and yell, *Boo*. "He gives me the creeps."

Not exactly cause for arrest. "Why is that?"

"I don't know. The way he never stops by or shows his face. It's almost like he's hiding something." She shrugged.

"Some folks like their privacy," Mika pointed out. She was playing devil's advocate here. Looking around, she wouldn't disagree this place was creepy.

"True. Me and my Buddy keep to ourselves mostly. But, you know, you give the occasional wave if you come across a neighbor driving down the same street. It's common courtesy in these parts." She said the words like everyone should know and be on board. Mika had grown up in a small town and she could attest to the fact Mrs. Lynn wasn't exaggerating. It was part of small-town charm. Friendly waves. People who smiled when someone passed by. Not observing local culture didn't make someone a criminal. Although, to be fair, it did make them suspect and an outsider. City folk?

"Is the person male or female, as best as you can tell?" Mika asked.

"Definitely male." There seemed to be no question in the woman's mind. Mika took note.

"How about the dog?" Mika asked.

"She's a sweet girl." She flashed her eyes. "Don't get me wrong, she'll bite in a heartbeat while protecting her territory. But she's not bad to the bone."

"What else can you tell me about her?"

"She seems friendly enough whenever I bring over food. I'm scared to death he's going to catch me and I don't stick around to see what happens. I drop the food and run." Her pale blue eyes widened when she said, "Gives me the willies just being over here."

Again, she glanced around, fidgeting with her robe and shifting her weight from left to right foot. Her actions were putting Mika on edge.

"Can you provide your landlord's information?" Mrs. Lynn was proving a goldmine of information. Maybe this case would be more cut and dried than Mika first feared.

"Yes, ma'am. I have it right here." She pulled her cell out of her front pocket and thumbed through her contacts, stopping on the name Elias Hunt. She held up the screen and Mika entered the information into her own cell. There was probably a way to hold the phones toward each other and make the transfer, but this was a new phone and Mika wasn't the most tech savvy person on the planet.

She preferred a simple life with less gadgets. The thought of a simple life, considering her mother's condition, would make her laugh if it was funny. Nope, her future was going to include doctor appointments and an uncertain future. How was that for funny?

Mika shook off her revelry. Time to focus on something she could help. The dog was going to get a better life, whether she knew it or not. Mika went to great lengths to make sure every dog that was confiscated found a forever home. It made the days at work longer and she used her days off to make calls, but seeing an animal that had been abused or neglected find a home, find people who would love and protect it, made every ounce of energy she put into the job worth it.

With her mom's condition, though, Mika was going to have to shift her priorities. She glanced over at the animal. Not before she found her a home. Mika could still take care of this girl.

"Thank you," she glanced up at Mrs. Lynn, who still had tears in her eyes. She seemed like a big-hearted person. One of the many reasons Mika loved small towns in Texas. Everyone should look after each other this way. Of course, there were always bad seeds, just like even the most well-tended and beautiful gardens had weeds. "Any idea what her name is?"

Mrs. Lynn shook her head. "I call her Sweetpea when I bring her food."

"Does she growl at you?" Mika figured it didn't hurt to ask.

"Sometimes. She seems protective of this..." Mrs. Lynn waved her arm in the air, "crap hole." She flashed eyes at Mika. "Pardon my French."

"No worries here." Mika gave a half-hearted smile. "I'm known for saying much worse."

That seemed to ease Mrs. Lynn's fears that she'd overstepped her bounds.

"I just get frustrated, you know?"

"Yes, I do." It was the whole reason Mika decided to do this job in the first place. Animals were so helpless. They were one hundred percent dependent on their people. Some didn't take the responsibility seriously or, worse yet, got dogs for all the wrong reasons. The closest thing to God in Texas wasn't family, it was football. The other thing Texans loved were their animals. In the case of the star lineman, the dogs came first.

She'd placed the sweetest bait dog in the care of a former U.S. Marine. He'd been injured, rehabbed, and came home with one robotic hand. Mika, who normally didn't do tears, cried like a baby when she saw the instant bond between those two. It was the whole reason she gave up weekends, and now that part of her was going to have to be put on the backburner to care for her mother.

Without being able to follow a case all the way through and make a real difference, this job held little appeal. Without that, she would have more heartache than happiness. It was exactly what got her through seeing an animal, like this girl, chained to a tree with little to no human or other animal contact. In fact, in these parts, it could also mark her as easy prey to a coyote or bear despite her size.

Even from here, it was easy to see she was a substantial girl.

"You already mentioned her protectiveness. Has she ever tried to bite you?" Mika asked, figuring she'd gotten about as much as she could from Mrs. Lynn.

"Never stuck around long enough to find out."

Those words weren't exactly encouraging. Mika would start with food and water so she could get close enough to assess the dog's threat.

"Well, I better get back across the street, unless you still need me." Mrs. Lynn was surveying the area carefully. Strange, because at that moment, Mika felt the sensation of eyes on her again.

"No, ma'am. You've been very helpful already."

The neighbor smiled before taking off, all the while looking around like she was a school kid trying to stay under the radar of the teacher while passing a note. Not exactly reassuring but Mika had that same creepy-crawly feeling from earlier. It was intensifying.

Now to see if Sweetpea was going to leave the easy way or the hard way. Mika had already filled out the form that needed to be taped to the window. She retrieved it from the vehicle and walked to the front door. Instead of removing the notice she'd place on there three days ago, she added today's notice to the window. She wished she could have gotten back here sooner. She was in the clear to seize the animal.

Looking around at Sweetpea's living conditions, once again Mika had to remind herself of the good that was coming for her. This was the low point. Never again would she be subject to this kind of neglect even if Mika had to take her in herself.

"Hey, sweet girl." Mika took the couple of steps toward the tree.

The animal moved. Nose wrinkled, ears back, and hackles raised, were signs of fearful aggression. And then she lunged. Mika fumbled back a couple of steps. The smell of fire wafted over her. Was it burning trash day?

As if her day couldn't get worse, the dog yelped as she bolted toward Mika again. The chain came loose from the tree, and the dog hauled past Mika. She tried to grab at the chain. It was short and she was too slow. A link must've given way. She hopped up and followed the dog. Letting her get away now while fearful could end badly for the animal. Mika's heart sank to her toes as the dog, even in a weakened state, disappeared into the tree line.

There was no way she could leave that dog to starve to death in the woods or, worse, become prey. She'd barely had enough food and water to keep her alive, and the little that she had had, was thanks to the neighbor.

Mika whistled as a crushing sense of sadness slammed into her. Following the sound of the heavy chain, which was surely the only reason Mika was able to somewhat keep pace with the dog, the tiny hairs on the back of her neck pricked.

"Hey there. Slow down." The strong male voice up ahead vibrated through her, sending heat swirling through her body.

She stopped mid-run, slowing her pace and biting back a curse. Her adrenaline spiked and her heart battered her ribcage from the inside out. All her senses snapped to full alert and her next steps were carefully planned.

Weapon drawn, she approached the stranger.

2

A large dog with a chain around its neck running like there was no tomorrow wasn't something Hayden McGannon normally saw while checking fences on his family's multimillion-dollar cattle ranch. This was a day for firsts.

With all the chaos at the ranch in recent weeks, nothing should surprise him.

"Hey, there. Whoa." He tried to soothe the frightened animal to no avail. All manner of things could happen with the chain attached to its neck. Tongue out, panting, the dog didn't look like it was in good condition. Just as he started to follow, movement caught his eye.

"Freeze. Hands up where I can see 'em." A female came into view. She stood behind a tree just enough to block everything but a sliver of her face and her gun. The business end was aimed directly at Hayden.

He did as instructed. Mainly, because she had the same law enforcement quality to her voice and based on the unusual circumstances with the dog, he figured she was on the chase. "If you're chasing a dog, it's getting away. We can do this dance a little longer and the animal will get too far to catch. Or you can step out on a limb and trust me. What will it be?"

"What are you doing out here in the middle of nowhere?" She surveyed the area and he realized she was looking to see if he had company. She was also out of breath, which indicated she must have been chasing the dog for a while.

"I'm out here working; this is a cattle ranch. I'm out here checking fences to make sure we don't lose any of our herd," he said. "It's part of my job. Now, since you're trespassing on private property, I need to ask your name and the nature of your visit."

"Officer Mika Taylor. I'm with animal control." She inched away from the tree and more of her face came into view. A lightning bolt struck Hayden square in the chest. She was a little taller than average height, around five-feet-five-inches if he had to guess. Her height was the only thing average about her. "Identify yourself."

"Name's Hayden."

The darkest brown hair without actually being black, parted on the left side, framed an oval-shaped face. Eyes like honey stared up at him as she moved closer. He dropped his gaze down to her rose-colored lips. Bad idea.

"That way." He pointed east, forcing his gaze away from her before he embarrassed himself. She had the kind of curves made for sinning and was most definitely off limits. Besides, his brother and all of his cousins may have found the real deal, but he wasn't drinking from that fountain anytime soon. No way. No how.

Despite the lightning bolt and feeling like this was different from anything else he'd experienced, Hayden believed in love at first sight about as much as he bought into the Tooth Fairy. Both were childhood whims.

"I'll go with you. You might get lost and we have a better chance of catching him together," he bit out.

"Her. It's a she." She mumbled something about it being easier to keep an eye on him if he tagged along.

"Got a name for *her*?" he asked, not bothering to hide the fact he was perturbed by the interruption to his work, to his day, and to his life. But then again, everything got under his skin lately and he needed to settle down.

"A neighbor called her Sweetpea. No idea what her owner named her. Wouldn't want to use the name anyway, after the way he neglected her." She took in the scene, blinked at him, and then holstered her weapon. He must've gotten the stamp of approval. He was, in fact, running fences. It was easy to see by the hammer tucked in his tool-belt. He took off his gloves and dropped them on the spot.

"Well then, let's get after it." He started in the direction of the dog, figuring there wasn't much chance they would catch up to her now. "Tell me the situation."

"She's probably weak from malnutrition. A neighbor has been sneaking her food and water but the owner disappeared and has been gone for days without checking on her." She stopped as she sucked in a few breaths as they picked up the pace to a jog.

The chain cut through some of the underbrush. Hayden followed the marks, tracking it like he was stalking a poacher, which was all-too-common of an occurrence on a ranch the size of his family's.

The animal cut a sharp left and Hayden knew exactly why she would do that. Water. There was a creek nearby.

"Hey, where are you going?" the enforcement officer said.

"You want to find her or not?" His words came out a little sharper than he'd intended.

"Wouldn't be here if I didn't." Good for her for not putting up with his mood.

"Just follow me." He didn't need a lot of reverb and yet he cracked a half smile anyway at her retort. Hayden had always respected strong women. Mika Taylor was proving to have the right kind of spunk to put him in his place. And he could almost hear her rolling her eyes back there.

She was a smart cookie too. Letting him take the lead meant she would always be behind him, watching him. He appreciated people who were good at their jobs. She seemed formidable and he couldn't knock anyone who stood up for animals for a living. A part of him that he tried to deny but couldn't wanted to get to know her better. How was that for the second surprise of the day?

"Do you normally work this area of the property?" she asked.

He put his hand back to keep her quiet, slowing his pace. Without another word, he crouched down, using his hand to tell her to follow suit.

The rush of water over rocks was just ahead. Something big and bear-like moved, and he thought of his cousin's dog, who'd been found face down along a creek on a different area of the property. The dog had appropriately been named Bear. The dog ahead would give Bear a run for his money in the size department.

Hayden inched forward, figuring any progress would be good. If she was tired and he could close the gap to a reason-able distance, there was a good chance she could be caught. The animal control officer was keeping a low profile. She was also being quiet, which he appreciated. He was, after all, trying to help her. And, to be honest, trying to help out the animal as well. Any creature that had been chained up for even part of her life hit him in the center of his chest. That was most likely the reaction he had earlier and not the gorgeous brunette behind him. So, why was his body tuned into her presence?

Way to keep emotions in check, McGannon.

In all honestly, his emotions had been all over the place since his father's arrest. Now, he found out two of his brothers were just giving up on the family and moving on. Moving out of state. To make tacos for God's sake.

Not that there was anything wrong with tacos. Hell, he loved tacos. But he'd worked side-by-side with all of his brothers and their decision to leave felt like rejection and the worst possible betrayal. So, yeah, he wasn't taking the news well. And, yeah, he was crabby. That tended to happen when his world fell apart around him and there was nothing he could do to stop it.

Dammit, he wanted his brothers to be happy. He also wanted them to be moving toward happiness and not running away from problems, which he suspected might be part of the timing of their decision. There wasn't a reason in the world they couldn't open a taco stand here in Cattle Cove. Especially since this is where everyone lived. This is where everyone *had* lived for their entire lives.

The girl dropped down next to the creek bed. No. No. No. She couldn't succumb. Hayden popped to his feet and started running. By the time he reached the dog, she was too exhausted to mount a fight. Make no mistake about it, she'd bite if she could.

He quickly assessed her condition. It was bad. He bit out a few curses as Mika dropped to the animal's side and gave her an injection.

"What is that?" he asked.

"A healthy dose of vitamins." She quickly went to work assessing the dog's health, pinching her skin. "She's severely dehydrated and malnourished."

"What will that shot do?"

"Probably give her enough energy to bite me."

Her honestly caused him to smile.

"Don't you die on me," she said to the dog, cradling her head as she scooted over.

"I'll be right back."

"Oh, no. You're not leaving my sight."

"I have a truck parked near where I was repairing fences. There's a way through the creek that will put me right there." He pointed to a spot about fifteen feet away.

She gave him a serious eye and he could tell she was deciding whether or not she could trust him. A glance down at the animal and she nodded. She seemed to realize it was the dog's best hope of survival.

"I'll be right back, Mika. You can trust me." He wasn't sure if it was the fact he used her first name or the level of seriousness he conveyed in his voice, but she looked up and half smiled.

"I really hope so, Hayden. Because her life depends on it."

Another bolt of lightning struck. At this rate, he would walk away looking like he'd stuck his finger in a light socket.

"I know."

THE GUY whose butt Mika was definitely not staring at way too long as he walked away, was either a saint or a serial killer. Since she had no personal experience to draw on for either, she went with gut instinct, which told her that he was a nice ranch worker who was trying to help her out while she was in a pinch. Maybe more importantly, a person who cared for animals not unlike herself. He'd seemed truly affected by Sweetpea's condition.

Mika almost rolled her eyes at the name for a hundred-plus pound dog. Sweetpea had to go.

She placed the dog's head on her lap. The sweetest, most innocent black eyes stared up at her. They were almost pleading. The animal had to know just how vulnerable she was and that Mika could do basically anything to her that she wanted.

"I'm not going to hurt you. We'll get you help," she soothed, stroking her matted fur as surprising tears welled in her eyes. She didn't normally get so choked up. What had gotten into her?

"Don't worry, sweet girl." Mika didn't want to startle the dog, so she stroked the fur of her face. "He'll be back."

Mika had no idea if those last words were true. She hoped. That was as far as she could go.

A few minutes passed before she heard the roar of the engine and the sounds of someone who was hauling butt to get to them. She didn't want her heart to batter her ribs at the thought of seeing Hayden again. She chalked her excitement up to the help she would be receiving for the dog and not the fact that his tall, male presence awakened every feminine part of her.

The guy had to be six-feet-five-inches of pure muscle. She guessed long hours working on a ranch would give a man the kind of body he had—the kind advertising agencies would put on a billboard in a major city like New York.

But, hey, no one would catch her complaining about the view. That was pretty much all he had working for him. So far, other than his soft spot for animals, he was pretty much a grumpy jerk. Definitely not her type. Although, she had no idea why she'd had the thought in the first place.

"You're okay," she soothed, stroking the matted fur. She hoped the animal realized she was there to help, not hurt. After seeing the conditions she'd been left in, there was no way she could trust humans. The kindness of the neighbor could make her slightly friendlier toward females.

The desperation in those eyes, though, was a real gut punch.

Hayden, the ranch hand, came bolting toward them. His presence stirred her heart in ways she also didn't want to notice or acknowledge. She couldn't afford an attraction or the burst of hope that came along with it. No one knew the future for certain. The only guarantee with her mother was decline. How fast? How it would all shake out was anyone's guess. Even doctors couldn't predict what the next twelve months would look like let alone a couple of years.

As he got close, she shifted the dog's head out of her lap. A moment of panic crossed those dark eyes.

"We're here to help you, sweet girl." The dog obviously couldn't understand the words, but Mika was convinced dogs understood intention. At least, once they got past the abuse and neglect. This girl was full-grown, if not fully filled out. The best outcomes usually came with the earliest interventions. Her cell was full of pictures from those success stories. And then there was the occasional lost cause. In her five-year career, there'd been three. Three too many if anyone asked her. A German shepherd, a pitbull, and a Chihuahua named Charlie.

"This is as close as I could get because of the trees." Hayden had a thick blanket tucked under one arm. "I thought we could use this as a sort of gurney to make it easier on her."

"Okay." Mika eased her hands out from under the dog. "I'll take the head."

Hayden shot her a surprised look.

"You sure about that?" he asked.

"A hundred percent." She couldn't risk a civilian taking a bite while helping her. In fact, she was going against protocol allowing him to get in close range at all. He could sue the department if he got hurt. He could sue the McGannons. She couldn't allow that to happen to such decent people. She'd heard nothing but good things about them despite never having the opportunity to meet anyone from the family personally.

"We're out of cell range here but if we can get her to the vet we can start immediate treatment," he said.

Considering it was the animal's best chance at survival, Mika wasn't about to refuse. She'd take all the help she could get on this one. With everything in her heart, she needed to avoid failure number four.

3

"On your count, we lift." Hayden was impressed with the animal control officer's commitment to saving the sweet dog.

"One. Two. Three." Mika wasted no time. She'd also nearly taken a bite when she scooped her hands underneath the big girl's shoulders, a risk many wouldn't have taken. And she seemed to have a calming effect on the animal.

They lifted on cue.

Growing up at McGannon Herd, Hayden had spent a lifetime around animals. He had enough experience to say this one was unpredictable. She was also weak. Her energy was drained with the run and she didn't have much fight left in her. A rescue with this girl could go either way, but the will to live or die was a powerful force. In some cases, an animal could have all the benefits of medicine but a weak spirit. Those times weren't especially successful and were frustrating as all get out.

This girl had some fight in her. Was it enough?

Despite being not much more than a bag of bones, she

was heavy. Hayden walked backward, since he knew the terrain the best and could keep his footing. He'd left the back door open to the dual cab truck. Climbing in while holding up the blanket was a feat in and of itself.

Between the two of them, they managed to secure the dog.

"I'll climb in back with her if you don't mind," Mika said. "Not a problem. There's a fresh water bottle on the floor. Maybe you can get some inside her." Hayden jumped in front, and then navigated back to the path. The vet's office was an hour and a half drive that was mostly spent in silence. The minute he was in cell phone range, he called the vet. Derek Jacobs had been with the family for years.

Despite the long drive, the dog was doing a little better by the time Hayden parked. It was most likely the rest combined with some hydration and the vitamin shot Mika had managed to give. "You got the chain from around her neck."

"Yes." Mika practically beamed. "She's doing slightly better now too."

Derek came running out with his gurney and one of his techs.

After exchanging quick greetings and introductions, Hayden helped Derek place the dog on the gurney.

"I'll take good care of her," Derek promised.

"I know you will."

The gurney disappeared into the building after a nod.

"Can I give you a ride somewhere?" Hayden asked.

"I'd like to stick around." She glanced at her phone. "It's almost time for my lunch break. I'd rather wait it out. Unless you have somewhere to be." She flashed honey-colored eyes at him. "Oh, you must. You probably have to get back to work. I don't want to get you in trouble with your boss."

Hayden nearly cracked a smile on the comment. "I'll be all right."

"You were in the middle of something." Her gaze unfocused like she was looking inside herself for the answer. "Mending fences."

"That, I was." He brought his hand up to lean on top of the door. "No one will miss me."

Her face twisted in confusion. "This bill is going to cost more than the county will be willing to pay. I'll just go in and tell the vet to bill me directly. Give him my credit card or something. Do you think he'd allow me to make payments?"

"The ranch will cover it. Don't worry."

Now, she really looked at him like he had two foreheads.

"You've been really kind. To her. To me. But, I seriously don't want to get you in trouble with your boss. I've heard the McGannons are an amazing family but this is probably going too far even for them." She had her hands up, palms out, like she was trying to physically stop him from making a mistake he couldn't come back from.

This time, he chuckled. Her eyebrow arched as he stuck his hand out between them.

"I don't think we were properly introduced earlier. My name is Hayden McGannon."

Her mouth nearly dropped to the floorboard. She mouthed an *Oh*.

"I thought you worked for the McGannons," she countered.

"I work at the ranch."

"Mending fences?"

"Everyone pitches in on a ranch. No one is above getting their hands dirty," he clarified.

It took a minute for her to speak. For a long moment, she just stared into space. Then, she nodded and smiled at him.

"Good to know and it explains why you seem so down to earth."

Her demeanor changed ever so slightly with the realization he was basically ranching royalty. Her gaze said she was quietly assessing him and he got the distinct impression she wasn't going to back down or away from him just because he was a McGannon. People acted different around him when they knew who he was. To be honest, he wasn't real fond of it. No one should be treated differently because of their last name or the amount of zeroes they had in a bank account. He definitely wasn't broke, but he also was fortunate not to have to care about his financial picture. There was a house with his name on it that he'd owned since turning twenty-one. A nice two story, modern log cabin with more bedrooms than he could possibly fill. It was the house of a younger man with his entire future in front of him. And a lot of help from Miss Penny, who had been there through every scrape and bruise alongside his uncle. The pair of them had stepped in to raise him while his father ran off to gamble away his inheritance. And the two of them had been there ever since.

Life had a way of changing courses, wanted or not. All a person could expect to do was try his level best to hang on no matter how twisty the road ahead became.

He'd hung on.

"If you don't mind, I'd appreciate it if you went back to talking to me the way you did when you thought I was a random ranch hand. Being a McGannon comes with a lot of perks. But notoriety isn't one of them." Don't get him wrong, he was grateful for the roof that had been provided over his head and the fact he never had to worry about where his next meal was coming from. He'd seen that particular pain firsthand and didn't wish it on his worst enemy. "I'm just an ordinary guy who just happens to have been born into an extraordinary family. Doesn't change who I am."

"No?"

"Not a bit."

"Good. Because I don't have a lot of friends who can afford fancy cars or big houses, so I have no idea how to talk to people like that," she said without skipping a beat. "I prefer normal. Normal is good. Normal works for me. So, if you're looking to be treated normal, I'm your person."

"Good," he parroted. "Glad we got that out of the way."

"Me too." The air had shifted but she was making an effort. She rolled her shoulders like she was rolling through the sudden tension that came with fearing she'd offended a member of a powerful family. He'd seen that before too.

"Now that we've established the fact I don't have to go back to work right now, what else can I do to help you?" he asked.

"Loaded question." Mika issued a sharp sigh.

He cocked his head to one side, figuring there was a story behind her response.

"You definitely don't want to hear my problems." In a rare moment since meeting her, he saw Mika let her guard down.

"You said you were on your lunch break. How about we grab a bite and you can tell me what's on your mind."

***

"I LOVE a place in town called DOUGH. Any chance you're in the mood for pizza?" It was probably a mistake for Mika to relax, but she was off her game and it would be so nice to talk to someone for a change instead of bottling everything up.

"As long as we're talking about a supreme." He glanced at the driver's seat and then back at her, looking distressed.

"Any chance we can have it delivered?" she asked, not wanting to leave the dog and figuring he was having the same response.

When he exhaled a breath, she realized she was on to something.

He stabbed his fingers through thick, black hair before reaching into his pocket for his cell. He scrolled through contacts and shook his head.

"I have the number," she offered. It was her favorite place to stop off whenever she came into Cattle Cove. She produced her cell. "I can make the call."

"I need to add it to my contacts anyways." He held out his cell. "Do you mind doing the honors?"

She took his cell and entered the information. She handed the phone back and then realized why he'd done it that way. He wanted to pay. Her purse was locked inside the county-issued vehicle. She started to offer to split the bill. One look said that wasn't a fight she would win. She could, however, pick up the next tab.

Next tab? What were they? Friends? No, they weren't. They didn't even know each other a couple of hours ago despite her heart trying to convince her otherwise. One look in his eyes said he was an old soul. She would leave it at that. Thank him for his generosity once the dog was fixed up and ready for a new home.

Speaking of which, Mika needed a name for the dog. She couldn't go around referring to her as 'the dog' or 'the animal' for much longer. And this one looked like she was going to be a longer-term investment.

Hayden ended the call with the pizza shop and then looked at her.

"Lady."

He cocked a dark brow.

"She needs a name." Mika nodded toward the building.

"It's a good name," he confirmed. It shouldn't make her heart dance, even though that's exactly what happened.

Since when did she need approval from a stranger? Except that Hayden McGannon—and she was still trying to adjust mentally to his last name—wasn't a stranger. Not anymore. They had informally met and now officially as well.

"Good. Then, I'll call her Lady."

"Any idea what's next for your girl in there?" he asked.

She scooted across the bench seat of the truck to make room for him, happy when he hopped in. The door was open, and the air was turning. The sun warmed her face just enough to stave off a chill.

"Not a clue," she admitted.

"Are you planning to keep her?"

"I don't have the room or the bandwidth," she said quickly. A little too quickly?

"Husband at home?" He glanced at her left hand and she could've sworn he sighed relief when he didn't find a band or a tan line.

"Not exactly. I do have family responsibilities, though."

"Kids?"

"Mother." Her sister was the one with the husband and three kids in Colorado. The situation made the burden of their mother's care rest on Mika's shoulders. "She was just diagnosed with a medical condition that's going to make caring for her become a full-time job."

"I'm sorry." Those two words spoken from a man she'd

met only hours ago shouldn't provide the amount of comfort they did. Warm campfires lit inside her as his voice traveled over her.

"It's okay. This stuff happens, right?"

"Unfortunately, it does. Doesn't make it any easier to deal with at the time, though." His insight seemed to come from a place of experience. Then she remembered reading about the McGannon family curse. Two brothers whose wives died tragically young and after having six and five children respectively.

"I'm just at the beginning of this road and, this probably makes me an awful person, but it's a lot to deal with. I'm not so sure that I'm the right person for the job. You know?"

"I can only imagine," he admitted.

"Sorry. We just met and here I am telling you my problems—"

"Don't be." He shook his head. "It's not good to hold it all in. Or, at least, that's what I'm told."

When he brought his gaze up and smiled a half-crooked smile through perfectly straight, perfectly white teeth, a dozen butterflies took flight in her chest.

4

A car wheeled into the parking lot. The driver wore a cap that Hayden recognized as part of the DOUGH uniform. "Looks like lunch has arrived."

When Mika smiled, the most amazing thing happened. A blush reddened her creamy skin and she looked even more beautiful.

"Good. I'm starving after all that running," she quipped, ducking her head. Was she deflecting? He hoped not because the world had been reduced to just the two of them and he never knew a parking lot could feel like the most intimate place in the world.

He waved the driver over and took the box from him.

"Would you like plates?" The driver strained to get a good look around Hayden.

Protective instincts kicked in and he shifted his weight to block the guy's view to Mika. Hayden glanced over his shoulder.

"I'm good eating out of the box if you are," she said. He liked a no-muss, no-fuss person when it came to eating. The two of them were going to get along just fine, he thought before he reined it in. First of all, they barely knew each other. Second, he wasn't in the market for anything serious and there was something about Mika Taylor that told him one night or dating with no strings attached wasn't in the playbook.

"Napkins only," he said to the driver, unable to contain his smile.

The driver held out a handful of napkins, which Hayden took.

"Thanks for the nice tip, by the way," the driver said, motioning toward the receipt taped to the box. "I appreciate it."

"Least I can do." Hayden wasn't obvious or showy with his money, but he knew what a hard day's work was and he always tipped generously to those who were willing to roll up their sleeves and put in a day's work. Those were typically the kinds of values handed down from a father to a son. In his case, it had been his uncle.

The driver nodded before pulling away. Pizza box in hand, Hayden returned to the truck and reclaimed his seat. He set the box in between him and Mika, and then split the napkins with her.

"This smells amazing." The 'mmm' sound she made caused him to think of better ways to make the same sound, ways that involved both of them naked and tangled in the sheets.

Since that thought—let alone that image—was about as productive as trying to milk a bee, he shoved it aside. Doing so took more effort than he thought it should.

So, he focused on his promise to LeAnne. That's all it ever took to douse the flame, no matter how brightly it burned. A voice in the back of his mind reminded him that he never allowed anything to get much beyond a spark. He was the shut-down king when it came to any relationship that showed promise.

Mika took a bite of pizza like it was her last meal. Again, he cracked a smile.

"I'm sorry about before," she said.

"Why?" He couldn't for the life of him place what she might be talking about.

"Not knowing who you are." She put a hand up to stop his protests. "I've heard really good things about your family's generosity. You guys do so much for animals in need."

Since she didn't want to hear that it was no big deal to him, he decided to take another tact.

"Good. If you truly feel that way, I was hoping you'd allow me to take Lady to the ranch to rehab her once she's cleared from Derek."

Mika didn't speak for a long, thoughtful moment. And then she nodded.

"I'd have to get it cleared with my SO." She glanced over at him and he must've shot her a look because she clarified, "Supervising officer."

He nodded, and then took another bite of pizza.

"Considering your family name, I doubt it'll be a problem. But there are protocols that have to be followed to make certain we dot every i and cross every t. I wouldn't want her owner to come back with a lawsuit or demand she be returned to him because we took a shortcut," she admitted.

"Playing by the book is good," he confirmed when she tentatively looked at him. "I wouldn't have it any other way."

And then she said, "I was actually thinking about keeping her at my home for at least a couple of days while my mom is visiting my sister in Colorado. I have the house to myself and as much as I want to curl up in bed for three days while I'm off duty, she might give me something to focus on." She flashed those honey-browns at him. "Idle mind..."

"...is the devil's playground," he finished when she didn't. The hint of sadness in her tone artfully covered by a jutted chin tugged at his heartstrings.

"You know that saying?" Her cheeks flamed and it was about the sexiest thing he'd seen in longer than he cared to remember.

"Doesn't everyone?" he said with a smile.

"I guess so. Most people at least. I had a co-worker who looked at me like I had six arms once." She laughed and her voice had a musical quality to it. One that made him want to sit up and listen to.

"Must not have been from around these parts." While they were on the subject, he wanted to know more about her, like where she was from and where she grew up.

"No. Definitely not."

"What about you? What makes you know sayings that float around here like leaves in the fall?" he asked, figuring it was a good segue.

"I'm from a small suburb north of Houston. My father worked in oil until the floor fell out. We moved after that. Downsized as people call it," she said in between bites of pizza.

"You mentioned a sister. Any other family?"

"Not anymore." She flashed eyes at him and for a split second he saw a lot of hurt there. "My dad decided my mom's diagnosis wasn't 'fun' enough for him to stick around." She rolled her eyes. "Sorry. I shouldn't be a jerk. He's still my father but I'm just so angry with him."

"What is going on with your mom? If you don't mind my asking," he quickly added.

"Early onset dementia." She cleared her throat and tucked her chin to her chest. He noticed she did that when she was trying to hide emotions when they got too intense.

"I'm sorry about your mother." Random and devastating illnesses hit a little too close to home.

He watched as the last slice of pizza became very interesting to Mika. She was the first person he'd talked to outside of the family in a very long time who made him want to learn more about her. She made him want to open up and talk about his past and the things going on in his life.

This realization wasn't something he took lightly. At the end of the day, he was so good at stuffing his emotions down deep that he wasn't sure he could manage to let them surface. Some were best kept locked away in a dark corner as far as he was concerned. No way in hell was he reliving that pain. So, why did a part of him *want* to open up and talk about it?

"Thank you," Mika said after a long pause. "I haven't really had time to process it all. My mom didn't want to 'burden' me with it when she first found out. As if her medical condition could be a problem for me. I guess she figured my dad would be there for her. That was the promise they made, in sickness and in health."

Hayden bit his lip to stop from speaking his mind about the kind of person who could leave his wife when she needed him most. Words wouldn't do justice to his thoughts anyway.

Though there was another side to him that could relate one hundred percent to having a father who turned out to be a huge disappointment.

"Were you close with him before all this happened?" he asked. At least his father had been honest about who he was from the get-go.

"He worked all the time while I was growing up. Then, he'd go out to dinner with colleagues or go for a beer, saying he was networking. My mom stayed at home." She shrugged. "He showed up to my high school graduation. Said he was saving up for the big events. My mom, on the other hand, was at everything. She came to every sport I played and cheered me on. In some ways, I think she threw herself into mine and my sister's lives to have a sense of purpose with my dad gone so much."

"She sounds like a loving mother." He didn't have many memories of his own.

"She was...*is*," she corrected. "And it's pretty unfair that she is the one who was struck by this illness while my dad gets off scot-free. By the way, he was having an affair with his administrative assistant. That's the real reason he left mom."

"Seems like he could have held off until your mom was on stable footing," he said and meant it. But then, he'd stuck around.

***

THERE WAS a quality to Hayden's voice that told Mika there was a story behind those words. She wasn't kidding before when she told him how much she appreciated his kind words about her mother. His comments were balm to a sore heart.

"Take it," he said as she looked down at the last slice of pizza.

"I couldn't eat another bite. And I've been talking way too much. I'm certain that I've bored you to death with my problems."

He slid the box toward her. "This might sound...weird... but watching you eat is a celebration of food. I can't tell you how many dates I've been on that..."

He shook his head instead of finishing the sentence. And a stab of jealousy nearly knocked the wind out of her at the thought of him on dates with other women. She chalked up her feelings to overwrought emotions about her mother's condition and the road ahead rather than entertain the possibility she could be jealous of women she'd never met before because they'd dated a man she barely knew.

It was strange that he felt so familiar to her, like they'd been close for years or knew each other in a past life. Twin souls? That was probably a stretch and she'd never believed in reincarnation but there was definitely something different about Hayden McGannon. Maybe it was the sadness she saw deep in his eyes that she related to on a soul-deep level. Either way, casting him as a stranger didn't feel right on any level.

"Good pizza," she said in the lamest response in the history of awkward moments.

"My favorite." He used the napkin before wadding it up. "I think it's a good idea for you to take Lady home with you for a couple of days. After, I'd still like to rehab her at the ranch. You'd be welcome to stop by any time to check her progress."

"I would like that. To see how she's doing." She leaned her head back on the headrest. "The best part of this job is watching an animal come through a terrible situation and ending up on top. Watching them get the happy home they deserve. It gives me hope."

When she looked at Hayden, he seemed to be studying her.

"What?" She suddenly felt bare, like he could see right through to her soul.

"It's nice to see someone who is so passionate about their job. Someone who throws everything they have into caring for something that can't look after itself. It's sweet."

For reasons she didn't want to examine or explain, she didn't want to be considered, 'sweet.' There was another 's' word that came to mind. Sexy. A small part of her wanted him to view her as sexy. The tan uniform she was wearing along with her hair in a ponytail probably wasn't helping matters.

Out of the corner of her eye, she saw the vet step out of the medical building and then come jogging over. His expression was serious and her heart sank. Out of instinct and nothing more, she reached for Hayden's hand as she braced herself the possible bad news.

The jolt of electricity should serve as a warning that getting too close to this man was a bad idea. But her heart went out to the dog and she was searching for comfort. His hand tensed when she made contact but then he relaxed and clasped their fingers together.

"What's the word?" Hayden asked his family's vet.

"She's severely dehydrated and underweight for her age," he began.

"Which is?" Hayden asked.

"Approximately three years old," the vet informed. "Physically, I can get liquids in her and I can bring her up to weight given enough time."

"But?"

"This is by far the saddest animal I've ever encountered. She doesn't trust anyone and her willpower is a concern."

"What are her chances of survival?" Mika asked. "If you had to put numbers to it."

"This is a tricky one. There's no medical reason why she can't survive. You mentioned that someone has been giving her food and water. It has been enough to stay alive. Her attempt to escape you took a whole lot out of her. She burned through what calories she had left. But, medically, her numbers are strong and this is survivable." He shook his head. "It would be a shame to lose someone so young just because she lost her fight."

Mika tightened her grip around Hayden's hand.

"Can we go in and see her?" Hayden asked.

"Of course. She's resting. I gave her a vitamin shot to boost her immune system, and she's receiving fluids. She's been given a low dose of pain reliever to help her sleep. You're welcome to stay as long as you like." The vet stepped aside.

Mika climbed out of the truck, taking the empty pizza box with her. Like a well-rehearsed team, Hayden was already gathering up the napkins. They tossed the items in the trash out front before following the vet inside. Once his hands were free again, Hayden immediately reached out. She liked the rough feel of his hands, hands that knew a good day's work.

The idea she'd had earlier of taking Lady home with her for a few days suddenly didn't seem as good as it originally did. Getting her used to one home only to change up her environment and caregiver a couple of days later didn't seem like the best thing to do.

Mika tugged at Hayden's hand. He stopped and turned around. Those eyes of his made her feel like she was standing on rubber.

"I changed my mind about taking her home with me. Under the circumstances, it's best if she goes straight to the ranch." She did her level best to cover the sadness in her voice that came with the admission.

He searched her gaze and her heart squeezed.

"Are you sure that's what you want?" he asked.

"It shouldn't be about what I want. Her needs have to come first."

Hayden didn't respond right away. Instead, he clenched his back teeth and the conceded.

"How about this. What do you think about coming to the ranch once your shift is over?" His offer was more than generous.

"Yes. I'd like that very much. If you're sure it won't be an imposition," she said quickly.

"You couldn't be." The deep timbre of his voice caused those words to wash right over her and through her. Her stomach free fell and she was certain about one thing. She was in trouble.

5

"**G**ood." Hayden took in a sharp breath. Staring into Mika's eyes much longer would be a mistake. "Let's go check on our girl."

He didn't wait for her to respond. Instead, he linked their fingers and walked into the exam room where Lady was on her side, sleeping. Walking up next to her, he could count her ribs. He flexed and released his fingers on his free hand, trying to work off some of the tension. There was never an excuse to abuse or neglect an animal. Only the lowest scum could intentionally hurt something that was so pure and so innocent.

He bit his back teeth so hard they might crack.

A couple of intentionally deep breaths later, and he was able to take another look at the animal. The knowledge her abuse stopped today was a big help in these situations. His family had helped rehabilitate dozens of animals over the years. Seeing them at intake never got easier or made his heart hurt less. Anger still ripped through him and he still wanted five minutes alone with the abuser. Let the person see what it was like to be at someone else's mercy for a change.

Hayden reminded himself that normal, healthy people would never hurt an innocent. The person had their own demons. He wasn't excusing their behavior in the least nor was he accepting it as okay. He was simply understanding in order to ease some of his pent up aggression.

As if sensing his frustration, Mika moved closer beside him. Electricity pinged between them with the force of a raging storm. It distracted him and caused him to shift gears, which probably wasn't a bad thing. He'd never experienced more chemistry with a person before, not even with LeAnne. Although, their love had been that pure, innocent love that knew no hurt. The kind of young infatuation that ran so deep, being away from the person for five minutes felt like an eternity.

Maturity and life experience put his relationship in a whole new light. And yet, first loves were the hardest to get over. This one, he reckoned, was impossible due to its extraordinary circumstances.

"Thank you for being so great today," Mika said, pulling her hand away and putting a little space in between them.

He must've shot her a confused look because her cheeks flamed again and that wasn't helping him with the whole attraction thing he had going on. Normally, thinking about LeAnne was all he needed to drain the liquid off any gas fire.

For the first time since he could remember, he wanted to think about someone else instead. He wanted to think about *Mika* instead. For reasons he refused to analyze, he picked that moment to pull his necklace out from underneath his T-shirt. A gold chain with his wedding band on it did what he couldn't. Shocked, Mika moved, turning her side toward him. Her body language as clear as a bell ringing, stay far away.

The necklace was a good reminder for him to keep his emotions in check.

"When can she be released?" Hayden asked Derek, who had been in the corner of the room standing and typing into a laptop.

"Normally, I'd want to keep her for a few days for observation. Knowing that you'll likely give her as good of care as we could, I'd say once I get another round of fluids in her. She collapsed from exhaustion and most likely had gotten overheated."

The air was chilly but the sun was strong. Having a black coat was a disadvantage here in Texas to be sure. He also knew that most dogs that ended up in shelters had black coats. They were also adopted less often for no other reason than the color of their fur. Shame, he thought.

Lady was beautiful. The thought of her being chained up outside was unthinkable to him.

"I'll give her a good flea dip before sending her on her way," Derek continued.

"Sounds like a plan." The chill in the room between Mika and Hayden was explainable, and his fault. Pulling his necklace out was normally all he needed to set his own mind straight when he felt himself going down a path with someone. It was rare, but it had happened. So, why did he feel like the biggest jerk in the world right now?

The apology he wanted to speak died on his tongue. The flash of hurt in Mika's eyes shouldn't bother him as much as it did. The instinct to pull her in his arms shouldn't be so strong.

So much for self-control.

Thankfully, Derek was still in the room. He was the great equalizer. Hayden could focus on his longtime family friend. He glanced at his cell. Several texts had come in. He'd been ignoring the real world since coming across Mika on the fence line a few hours ago. Although he didn't answer to anyone on the ranch, he did feel a responsibility to check in. It was common courtesy to keep each other updated and there was a safety element as well. There were too many cell phone dead spots on the land. Then there were poachers, wild animals, and other dangers to consider, especially since they spent a lot of time out on the property alone.

With all the drama going on in the family, he and the two brothers who were sticking around were becoming especially close. It was strange to think of cousins teaming up against cousins when they'd all grown up as brothers. Don't even get him started on the brothers who were ditching the family and the ranch they all loved now that life had become complicated. For tacos?

Checking the time, he asked, "How long before she's ready to go home?"

"Give me another hour or two," Derek said.

"That should give you enough time to take me back to my vehicle," Mika said. Her tone was all business now.

"Whatever you want." He motioned toward the door.

Mika didn't hesitate. She turned and walked out the door, not stopping until she reached the passenger door of his truck. He clicked the key fob, and she opened the door and climbed right in before securing herself with the seatbelt.

The cold air had nothing on the chill inside the vehicle as he claimed the driver's seat. Good. He couldn't regret bringing out his secret weapon. The necklace would stop him from making a big mistake. The necklace would keep him grounded. The necklace would stop him from hurting her, however unintentional.

She rattled off an address, and then stared at her phone for the entire ride. It was probably the longest forty-five minutes of his life. He pulled up next to the county-issued vehicle and put the gearshift in park.

"Thank you," Mika muttered as she practically flew out the door before he'd come to a good stop. He rolled down the window on the passenger side as she made a beeline for her white service vehicle.

"The offer to come check on her tonight still stands," he said louder than he'd intended.

Mika stopped with her hand on the door handle. She didn't turn around. "I'll keep that in mind."

Hells bells, he didn't expect her snub to sting as much as it did. They both knew she wasn't coming over.

For the first time with a new person, Hayden doubted himself. Had he done the right thing by pushing her away?

The only answer he could come up with was a resounding yes. If his heart and mind betrayed him this much in a couple of hours, think about the hay-day it would have if he spent a whole evening with her, despite the fact he was already mulling over what he could possibly cook for her.

Miss Penny kept his fridge stocked whether he wanted her to or not. He didn't discourage her. He'd learned a long time ago there was no 'off' button for a good parent. The operative word being *good*. One that actually *wanted* to become a parent. That was the defining difference.

Speaking of family, he needed to return a few texts. He put the gearshift in reverse, figuring he could wait out the

last of the IV treatment and the flea dip while sitting in the
parking lot of Derek's practice. He also realized he hadn't
stopped for five minutes since learning about his brothers'
decision to ditch the ranch.

Damn, that hurt. It was most likely that—and not the
fact he'd developed real feelings for Mika in such a short
time—that put a hole in his chest.

Even so, watching her drive away was a gut punch.

MIKA BLINKED BACK TEARS, wondering why in heck's name
she was suddenly turning into a leaky faucet. Hayden
McGannon was a married man. Or was he? The ring wasn't
on his finger. It was more like a keepsake dangling from the
necklace. Either way, she had no business pining after him
like a hormonal teenager in puppy love.

Was that the case?

Reason said it couldn't be. She'd barely known him five
minutes despite the nagging feeling that was a gross
underestimation. The irrational part of her that defied
logic said they knew each other. How could that be when
she would never have guessed he was married in the first
place?

Her mind warned that he could wear the ring there so
he wouldn't lose it. His job required putting gloves on and
off at times. What a complete fool. She'd been practically
tripping all over herself from how gorgeous he was, which
totally made sense now if he was committed to someone
else.

An annoying voice in the back of her head argued he
couldn't be. His family was known for being honest and
honorable. He seemed to care about the well-being of an

innocent animal. Could someone decent and kind be capable of a flirtation while he was married?

There were plenty of explanations as to why he'd be wearing a wedding ring on a necklace around his neck. His mother had tragically died when he was a young boy. Did the ring belong to her?

Mika gripped the steering wheel a little tighter than usual, to the point that her knuckles went white and her fingertips tingled from blood loss.

The mental debate needed to stop, so she refocused on her work. The cold front was moving in and she wanted to get home to her jacket. Of course, thinking about work brought up Lady.

Mika was most definitely not going to the McGannon ranch tonight. Doing so would be a mistake. Married. Not married. Single. Dating. In a committed relationship. Hayden's status had nothing to do with her. A fling would have been nice. Something to take the edge off and provide a distraction before her real responsibilities of caring for her ailing mother kicked in.

Her shoulders drooped forward and she exhaled like a balloon whose air had been let out. Maybe she could get a dog. Not Lady, but a lap dog. Taking on more responsibility at home didn't seem like the smartest choice but she finally *would* be home more. Every night and weekend except the few occasions when her sister could carry some of the load. Melanie warned she wouldn't be able to help out as much as she wanted to. The timing of their mother's illness wasn't stellar.

But then, when was it ever a good time to be sick? Or need help?

Plus, in some ways, Mika had shouldered the responsibility of their mother all of her life. Melanie had gone out of state to university, whereas Mika went to two years of community college in order to be closer to her mother since her father was gone so much of the time. She'd encouraged her mother to find something that interested her and join a club. Her mother had responded by swatting at her like she was shooing away a fly. She'd tell Mika how happy she was being home with her cooking and gardening. She'd remind her that Mika's dad was considering early retirement so they could buy a Winnebago and tour the country.

Mika nearly pulled her own hair out in those conversations. She'd known all along that her father wasn't ready to scale back work. He was only saying that to pacify his wife when she asked if they could spend more time together. It was always going to be later. Later when he got enough time in at the office to retire comfortably. Later when he saved up enough money to buy the Winnebago. Later when he had their future mapped out.

Later. Later. Later.

Well, look there. Mika hadn't thought about Hayden McGannon in the past five minutes since she went on a rant about her selfish father.

By the time her shift was over, she'd ticketed another five houses and pushed thoughts of Hayden McGannon out of her mind at least a dozen times. She might not be winning in that department, but she made it through her shift, turned in her vehicle, and headed home.

She was so tired, mentally and physically, her bones ached. If she drew a warm bath when she got home, she might not ever get out of it. Instead, she would opt for a shower and a takeout menu. Walking into her house, she pitched her keys in the bowl by the door and looked for her jacket on the back of the chair in the living room. It wasn't there.

That was weird. She could have sworn she left it there this morning. Blaming the fact she started her job at six o'clock in the morning wouldn't do any good. She'd worked the schedule for a solid year now. And, yes, she was still tired in the morning.

If she didn't leave her jacket on the chair, then where was it?

She skimmed the room. Nothing.

It was probably the day she'd had but the creepy-crawly feeling of eyes on her returned. She was creeped out enough to go back and lock the front door, something she rarely ever did before bed. In these parts, it wasn't uncommon to leave her windows open all night on a rare cool evening.

Had she locked her car? She retrieved her keys from the bowl she kept on a table near the front door, and then hit the key fob. The click-click noise was the confirmation she needed. She tossed the keys back into the bowl and resumed her search for the missing jacket.

Her memory had been bad lately. Ever since the doctor's visit, she'd been misplacing things. Or course, it didn't help that her mother had moved in. At times, Mika was one hundred percent certain her mother moved stuff around without even realizing what she was doing. That accounted for at least some of the missing items.

The jacket wasn't in the kitchen either. She checked the hall closet and came up empty.

The two-story house had three bedrooms. The master was upstairs along with a secondary bedroom that Mika used as an office. Downstairs, housed the living room, kitchen, and a guest bedroom, aka her mother's room. There was a half bath in the hallway along with a hall closet. The guest room had its own en suite. An enclosed back porch rounded out the place. She loved it. The rooms were good size. It was an older house which basically meant she had larger closets. The street out front was lined with mature oaks and mesquite trees.

The cul-de-sac kept traffic to a minimum and yet she felt like she still lived in a neighborhood with a quarter of an acre yards. It was perfect for her. A little bit tight with her mother there, but they could make it work.

Mika had a vision of navigating her mother through a divorce during what had to be the worst time in her life. The stack of papers waited in Mika's office. She should probably use her time off to dig in and see what her father was proposing in terms of a settlement. Texas was a no-alimony state, and for some reason, she didn't think her father was going to come through with a decent offer.

She blew out a sharp sigh, wishing for a minute that she could just disappear. Live on a beach somewhere. Collect shells for a living. That had to be a job. Right? If couples on those home renovation shows had a million-dollar budget to work with, but their jobs were supposedly to come up with new colors for crayons, someone would pay her big bucks to collect and paint shells, right?

Now, she really was getting loopy.

Still, the jacket situation was bothering her. Had she taken it to her car this morning without realizing it? She walked into the living room and grabbed her keys. Out the front door she went, doing her level best to shake off the creepy feeling from earlier.

It wasn't working but then she didn't really expect much with the way life was going. She wasn't feeling sorry for herself either. Crappy things happened to people all the time. Some got much worse. She was just tired and in a mood. One she was allowed to have for the next few days while she was off work.

Then again, sulking around the house on her precious time off suddenly didn't sound like such a great idea. Her mind snapped to Hayden McGannon as she searched the backseat of her car. Not there. The trunk was next. Not there either. So far, she was zero for two in the car department. And the creepy feeling that she couldn't shake had her feet moving towards her front door in a heartbeat.

6

M aking certain Mika locked the door behind her, she exhaled once she was back inside. Who knew where the darn thing was. For all she knew, she might have left it at the office.

She checked that she had locked the front door, something she was determined to do now that she was alone and couldn't shake the eyes-on-her feeling. She was being paranoid and she knew it. The knowledge didn't change how she felt. At least she recognized when she was being over the top. And, yes, emotional. And, yes, feeling sorry for herself a little bit. But mostly, feeling sorry for her mother.

Upstairs, she started to strip off her clothes on the way to the master bedroom at the end of the hall. When this house was built, there was no en suite for the master. Her bathroom was large and serviced both bedrooms. Since her second bedroom was an office, she didn't have to share with anyone. Basically, having the entire floor to herself was nice. She didn't realize the brilliance of making the upstairs bedroom into her office until her mother moved in. Having her own floor was definitely going to be a bright spot.

By the time Mika reached her bedroom, she was down to her bra and panties. She located her cell and chucked it onto the bed, tossing her work clothes in the door next to the closet. One of the coolest features of this old house was the laundry chute. There were no basements in Texas due to the shifty clay soil, so clothes went to the first floor that was attached to the laundry room off the kitchen. The room was clearly an add-on but she didn't mind. The past owners had done an excellent job with the reno project. Plus, having indoor laundry was a luxury she hadn't expected in a house this age. She figured she would be sacrificing a little bit of convenience for character and strong bones.

For reasons she couldn't explain in the context of this conversation in her head, she thought about Hayden again. He would have brought Lady home hours ago. Was she doing okay? Had she perked up after receiving fluids?

Those sad and weary eyes of hers were etched into Mika's memory. She had no doubts about how well Hayden would take care of the sweet girl. Would it be enough? A hole the size of Amarillo pierced Mika's chest thinking about Lady. Why? She was in good hands now. She was going to have a better life than most humans. So, why did Mika's heart ache for the animal?

Her cell buzzed. She glanced at the screen. She didn't recognize the number.

It could be Hayden.

She was keenly aware of how undressed she was in that moment. How had he gotten her number...oh, wait. She remembered him asking for her information for the dog. He was probably just checking to make sure the owner hadn't called, riling up her boss or something.

Covering herself with the duvet, she answered the call.

"Sorry for the interruption," he started. His deep masculine voice traveled over her, warming her uniquely feminine places. Her arms goosebumped.

"It's fine. I was just about to get in the shower."

A moment of hesitation on the line had her thinking she'd overshared.

He cleared his throat before continuing, "I thought you might want an update on Lady."

"I do. Thank you," she said quickly. A little too quickly. Her nerves were getting the best of her and she was doing a lousy job of hiding the fact.

"She's home. Still a little leery of me. I figure it'll take time after what she's been through." His voice sounded a little raw and husky, and a part of her wished she was having the same effect on him that he had on her. But the cynical side said he was probably having allergy issues.

"I can't imagine a better place for her to be. It was amazing of you to take her in like that," she said and meant every word.

"It's nothing any decent person wouldn't do." He brushed it off like it was nothing, but it most certainly was something. A big something. Not many people would open their home and their hearts to an animal that may never be able to love them back in the same way. It took a special person to rescue an animal. His family did it like it was nothing, but it meant the world to every single animal that went through their front gates. And he needed to know how special that made him in her eyes.

"Maybe I've been on the wrong side of humanity considering my job but I would beg to differ. You're going to make a huge difference in Lady's life." Her voice started to shake. Why was Mika getting so choked up?

"I appreciate hearing you say it." His voice was so low she almost didn't hear him. "She...I...would like you to know the offer to stop by still stands. And just to make it irresistible, I'm throwing in dinner. But before you get too excited, you should know that I don't cook."

"Good. I don't either."

"What do you think? Lady here would love to see you again. It might perk her up. She isn't yet responding to me," he admitted.

After being neglected, she might have a healthy suspicion of men. "If Lady is the one requesting it, I don't see how I could refuse."

Besides, the thought of eating dinner alone in her house had lost its appeal. Without another person there, the place felt a little hollow. The paperwork on her desk could wait and going to Hayden's would insure there'd be no temptation to work when she should be relaxing. "Let me grab a shower and then I'll head over. Should I pick something up for dinner on my way?"

"No. Miss Penny makes sure our fridges are stocked despite us being grown men who are capable of figuring out how to feed ourselves. She's been taking care of us since we were knee high to a grasshopper, so we don't complain. She's been too good to us and her cooking is better than any restaurant I could ever get to."

"I wouldn't mind having someone look after me for a change." Did she say that out loud?

His chuckle came from deep in his chest. It didn't help with the goosebumps or the warmth swirling low in her belly.

"And, Mika?"

"Yes?"

"If it's okay with you, it'd be great if you could stop mentioning you in the shower. It's putting all kinds of images in my head that don't belong there."

Didn't that light a dozen fires inside her. Electricity shot through her, igniting places that had been long dormant. She thought about his supposed wife. He couldn't be married now. Something must've happened or there were extenuating circumstances. He wasn't the kind of person who would say something like that if he was still married.

She cleared her throat and tried to find her voice. "Done."

After that, she ended the call, figuring she didn't need to open her mouth and insert her foot inside any more than she already had. Because now the image of him naked and in the shower was something she couldn't shake from her thoughts.

HAYDEN HAD BEEN home for hours, pacing in his kitchen. His restless mood couldn't be helping his new guest settle in. He'd gone over the necklace stunt in his head half a dozen times. Why then? Why couldn't he just let himself get to know someone? Why couldn't he put that part of his past behind him?

The answer was simple and yet more complicated than he wanted it to be. He wasn't ready to move on.

His cell buzzed in his hand, startling him. He wasn't normally caught off guard by much but lately...

His brother Coby was calling.

"Hey. What's up?" he answered.

"Nothing. Just checking in with you to see how you're doing." Coby and Reed had been in touch more recently since the news of their two brothers broke.

"I need to take a couple of days off work actually."

"Everything okay?" Coby's quick response reminded him how on edge everyone was.

"With me. Yes. I rescued a dog and she needs a couple of days with me twenty-four-seven."

Coby released a slow breath. "For a minute there I thought you were about to drop another bomb."

Everyone was on edge with their father in prison.

"I know we never talk about this but I just spoke to Reed. Has he told you about his meeting with Dad?" Coby asked.

"The one before Uncle Clive's so-called accident?" Hayden asked but it was rhetorical. "Where Dad wanted him to help take over the ranch?"

"That's the one." The disappointment and uncertainty in Coby's voice was uncharacteristic. But then, they'd all been thrown for a loop. "What are your thoughts?"

"Are you asking if I think he did it?" It was a hard question because he didn't like the answer that immediately came to mind.

"Do you?"

"I don't want it to be true. How about that for an answer?" It was a copout. None of Donny McGannon's sons wanted him to be the kind of person who could stoop that low. The kind of person who could plot against the brother who'd taken him in when he'd come crawling back.

"It's honest." Coby was letting him off the hook, and Hayden was grateful.

"How about you?"

"After talking to Reed, I'm convinced he's guilty," Coby admitted. "I wasn't sure before. But now that I know he was plotting against his own brother and trying to involve his son, I can't put my head in the sand and say there's a line he wouldn't cross."

"He has crossed a lot of lines no one should," Hayden

admitted.

"You want company tonight? I could use a beer."

"I-uh." The moment of hesitation, the stutter, wasn't something Coby would miss.

"Oh, right. I'll take a raincheck then," Coby quickly recovered.

"Are you sure? Because if you need to talk, I'll cancel." His heart clenched at the thought, but he would be there for his family over his own wishes. Because his wishes were to see Mika again and soon.

"No. Don't do that. I'll feel like a jerk," Coby said. "Tell you what. Next time. It's probably best for me to lock in tonight and finish up the paperwork on the pregnant heifers. In a few short months we'll be tagging a whole slew of new calves. Better to get started on all this now. Get ahead of the game."

"True. I can help once I get situated." Coby was reaching for an excuse but Hayden appreciated his brother for it. If the shoe were on the other foot, he would've done the same. And a sense of relief washed over him that he didn't need to cancel the night he was looking forward to more than he wanted to admit to his brother or to himself.

"No rush." Coby hesitated. "I hope you won't take this the wrong way."

Those words got Hayden's attention. "Okay."

"Let yourself have a good time tonight."

"Don't wo—"

"I'm serious. If anyone deserves to have a good time, it's you." The words sat heavy in the air for a long moment. The weight of them was centered squarely on Hayden's shoulders.

"I'll do my best." It was all he could promise.

"That's all I'm asking," Coby said, a hopeful note to his

voice. "She's been gone a long time now."

"You know what? I have to go," Hayden needed to rush his brother off the call. He didn't want to go down that road tonight—the one that made him think about her. He was doing his level best to shut her out of his thoughts and had mostly been succeeding.

"Okay." Coby had said his piece and Hayden hoped his brother could leave it alone now.

With a long exhale, Hayden let out the breath he'd been holding. His brother wasn't trying to dredge up those sad memories. Coby's heart was in the right place.

"Thanks, though. Your concern means a lot," Hayden said to his brother.

"We always have each other's backs. Remember?" It went without saying but was still reassuring to hear.

"That's right." He also realized how that didn't seem to apply to two of their brothers any longer. They were turning their backs on the family at the precise moment they needed to be able to count on each other. "But when did everything get so messed up that we had to band together?"

"I hear you, bro." Coby paused for another thoughtful moment before saying, "I'm pretty sure it happened the minute our father came back to town."

"There's a lot of truth to that statement," Hayden agreed. He would've mentioned it himself except that he was trying to go easy on the man. Why, though? What had their father ever done to deserve their grace? Their trust?

Not a whole heckuva lot.

"This stuff with Dad is a bump in the road. Uncle Clive knows us. He would never blame us or shut us out because of something Dad did or didn't do. They've been brothers since before any of us were a thought. Dad isn't pulling the wool over our uncle's eyes one bit," Coby said.

"Did you see how strongly Uncle Clive is trying to cover for Dad, though? He gives him the benefit of the doubt in every situation," Hayden pointed out.

"True."

Maybe Uncle Clive did know his brother. It wouldn't take much to know the man better than his sons did. Hayden and his brothers didn't have enough history with their father to know him on any level other than surface.

"You really think a man could walk away from his children and somehow not end up being the calloused jerk we believe he is? Because I'd like to hear your reasoning if you do," Hayden's stance was harsh. He realized it. Call it protecting being down to the basics of keeping himself from getting hurt, but he had to keep his guard up around their father. Life experience had taught him that some people were givers and some were takers. His father was clearly a taker.

"For one, he didn't just leave us with anyone. He left us with his older brother, a man who had a proven track record raising boys and who was better in pretty much every way than Dad was."

"He couldn't have left us in better hands," he agreed.

"Once he did that, he stepped aside. He didn't try to confuse us by showing up and trying to take back the role of being a father," Coby pointed out. "Which, by the way, doesn't mean I'm a big fan of his. I'm just pointing out the few things he got right."

"Point taken." Hayden thanked his brother for sharing his point of view and then ended the call.

Coby had given Hayden a lot to think about. But, right now, he wanted to focus on the person coming to visit. He wanted to think about Mika.

7

Fresh from the shower, Mika squirted her favorite date-night spritzer on her body before dressing in a lacy minidress. She threw on a faded denim jacket and pulled out her tan and teal cowgirl boots. Being from Texas, she'd grown up riding horses, but these boots were for show.

She let her long hair stay loose around her shoulders, tucking one side behind her ear. As she grabbed her cell phone and headed down the hallway, she glanced inside her office. Her jacket was in a pile on the floor.

Is that where she'd left it? Strange, because she couldn't remember the last time she'd brought it upstairs with her. It stayed down in either the closet or where she believed she'd left it. Then again, she was losing her mind lately. She might have absently brought it up with her and hung in on the doorknob. It could've fallen and ended up where it was now.

That, or her mother could've brought it upstairs, forgot why she'd made the trip, and then tossed the jacket inside the office. Things were showing up in all sorts of weird places now that Mika had a 'roommate.' Was that the term her mother had used when she'd shown up with four suit-cases and a trunk, asking for a place to live after her husband of thirty years kicked her out of their home?

But she didn't want to focus on that right now. Being angry would only muddle her thoughts. She needed to be clear-headed. She grabbed the jacket and headed down-stairs, closing the office door behind her out of habit. That was another oddity. She rarely ever left the door open.

Under normal circumstances, she wouldn't think anything of either of those two things. The two combined, and with the creepy feelings she'd been experiencing lately, she wasn't so sure she should sweep them under the rug.

She made a mental note to always make certain she locked her doors and to check the windows. Starting upstairs, she swept her bedroom, the office, and the small hole of a window in the shower area, locking the couple that were routinely opened.

Downstairs, every window was locked except one, the one to the laundry room. Not surprising because the A/C wasn't as strong in there and during the fall, she often kept the window open to let some of the heat out. Locking was new. But necessary. A small sacrifice for peace of mind.

After securing the front door, she walked to her vehicle with her shoulders a little bit straighter. This break was going to be just the ticket to get her mindset in the right place. She could feel it already. She could handle anything thrown her way and would. Figuring out the details might be tricky but her mother deserved to be taken care of after everything she'd done for Mika and her sister Melanie, not to mention how she'd cared for her husband all these years.

Settling in for the long drive, Mika noticed the sunset. Really noticed. On the highway that stretched on for miles, she could see nothing but wide-open skies and straight road for miles ahead. It was one of the things she loved most about Texas. The expansiveness of it. The blanket of stars that dotted a velvet night sky, a canopy of bright night stretching over the earth in all its splendor. That was one of many reasons she could never see herself living anywhere else. Texas was a home unlike any other.

Why didn't she sit outside every evening with a glass of wine or cup of tea in her hand and look up?

Funny how it took a life-changing event to change perspective. To make her see the beauty she'd been taking for granted all these years. She couldn't remember the last time she sat back and watched the sun rise or set. Being able to be outside was one of the many reasons she'd taken this job. And yet, she was just now realizing how little she allowed herself to stop long enough to enjoy it.

That was about to change, she thought as she turned on her favorite radio station. Garth Brooks was playing. *The Dance.* She loved that song. A vision of her and Hayden outside dancing in the moonlight struck.

Now she really was going crazy.

She glanced in the rearview and caught a look at her eyes. She'd put on a little liner. And she sure was gussied up.

An embarrassing thought struck. What if this wasn't a date? What if he really did just want her to come over and check on Lady? What if she'd gone to all this trouble to look nice when she would have been better off in jeans and a T-shirt? What if he really was married? No. No. No. Couldn't be. Her mind couldn't fathom it.

Just like everything in her life lately, she'd have to cross that bridge when she came to it. He did mention dinner. And she *did* feel like putting on a dress. She hadn't put on date-worthy spritzer in too long, and that was the reason she'd gone all out.

Plus, being realistic, she wasn't going to be dating a whole lot in the very near future. So, whether Hayden wanted to be on a date or not, that's what he was getting.

She thought about the wedding ring and her shoulders deflated. Since she was a rip-the-Band-Aid-off type, she would straight up ask him about the ring before taking a step inside his front door. If he said yes, she would hightail it out of there so fast it would make his head spin. Once she got off his property, she would pull onto the side of the road and find a restaurant or, better yet, bar. She had no plans to waste date-night spritzer without doing some flirting.

The conversation in her head lasted most of the ride over. When GPS estimated she was about fifteen minutes out, the panic really set in. The last thing she wanted to do was embarrass herself in front of one of the most influential families in the state. And generous. They were generous to a fault, taking in all manner of animals needing a home and a second chance.

Lady, girl, you just hit the jackpot. All she would have to do was look around, and she would perk up. Hayden's words about her sad eyes brought Mika's date-panic down to a manageable level. The sweet girl had better hang on and pull through. Her life was about to be so amazing. All she had to do was find the will to survive.

Out of nowhere, a deer sprang out front behind the tree line and darted across the road. Mika stamped the brake a second too late. She careened into the animal. Her car went into a tailspin. Her tires struggled to gain purchase. Her airbag deployed.

The vehicle jerked to a stop, causing her side airbags to deploy and her neck to snap sideways.

She wasn't sure how many seconds—minutes?—passed before she regained her bearings. Her hands burned a little bit. She glanced down, taking inventory of her body. No blood. Nothing broken. She was frustrated, not hurt.

And then she thought about the deer. It took some doing, but she managed to unsnap her seatbelt. Her hands shook, making the job twice as hard as it should have been. In fact, a slow tremor rocked her entire body as she pushed out of the car. Her legs didn't feel like they'd hold her weight, so she grabbed the top of her car.

Another quick inventory said she'd made it through in one piece. Shaken up? Yes. But physically fine. On the road, however, was the lifeless deer.

A tear broke loose but she quickly wiped it away, refocusing on her car. The front was mangled. There'd be no driving it. From the looks of it, she might be looking at structural damage. She'd have to wait word from her insurance company but a visual scan said the car was totaled.

She was in a little bit of shock. But she was also stuck.

Once again, the feeling of eyes watching her made the hair on the back of her neck stand up. Like someone was closing in on her. A noise in the underbrush caused her to jump. Her hand immediately went over her heart as if she could stop it from pounding her ribs.

Smoothing out her dress, she calmly walked over to her car. She grabbed her purse and set it on top of the hood of her car.

The rush of wind through the trees sent her pulse jackhammering. Was she really going to start jumping at every sound?

She flexed and released her fingers a couple of times to get the blood flowing and work off some of the tension. What did she need to do first?

Her date. She needed to call Hayden to let him know she wouldn't be able to make it after all. It was probably for the best. That man was dangerous for a whole other set of reasons. It was probably fate stepping in with this car crash, stopping her from doing something she might regret later.

Okay. Cell phone. Where was her cell phone?

She dug around in her purse, located it. It took a couple of tries for her thumbprint to work. She would laugh at the fact she lived in a small town for the safety of it except that now she was locking everything and double-checking locks. It wasn't funny.

Hayden. She refocused and pulled up his name in her contacts.

He answered on the first ring.

"Everything okay?" he asked.

"Not really." She didn't want to be a downer but she figured she'd come right out with it. "I crashed into a deer. My car is going to have to be towed. I'm sorry, but I need to cancel and deal with this...mess."

"I can help with that. Where are you?" His tone was all business. Rancher helping near-stranger. One of his many good traits.

"According to GPS I'm fifteen minutes out from your ranch," she said.

"And you were coming in from the southeast, correct?"

"Yes."

"Then, I have a pretty good idea of where that would put you," he said.

"You do?"

"First of all, I grew up here and never left. Second of all, there's only one road that'll take you to the ranch when you're within half an hour," he explained. "I'll be there to pick you up as soon as humanly possible and I'll send a couple of the guys to get your car."

"Are you sure?" she asked. "Because I can call roadside assistance. I have a plan."

She was starting to think more clearly as the initial shock wore off.

"Then I wouldn't get to see you tonight," he said. "And I would very much like to."

Her heart gave a little flip.

"Just don't go anywhere. The cavalry will arrive shortly. And you might want to sit inside your car with the windows rolled up until someone arrives to help," he said.

"Why?" An icy shiver raced down her spine at the suggestion.

"Mosquitoes. They'll eat you alive this time of year."

"Right." She rarely ever got out at night. She'd have to remember the mosquitoes when she sat on her porch with a glass of wine once her mother came back and she figured out her new normal.

A rustling sound coming from the nearby underbrush caused her to jump into the driver's seat, slam the door shut and hit the key fob to lock herself inside. *Holy smokes.*

"What's wrong?" Hayden's voice cut through the terror vibrating through her. Between her mother's situation, the O'Rourke case, and Jimenez's threats, she was starting to lose it.

She skimmed the trees. Unfortunately, her headlights weren't much help with the direction her car faced.

And then the call, her lifeline, cut off.

HAYDEN, in his vehicle and driving like a bat out of hell, gave the voice command to call Mika. In this part of the ranch, cell service was spotty. He bit back a few choice words and issued a sharp breath. Not knowing what was happening with her brought him back to a dark time in his life—a time when medical doctors became routine and the unknown was just part of the deal.

Didn't matter how many times he reminded himself this was a totally different situation. This was not LeAnne. This was Mika. He instinctively reached for the necklace, keeping his left hand on the wheel. He fingered the gold band and then rolled it between his thumb and forefinger.

A dozen curse words ran through his mind. So much pent-up frustration with no release. There could be no release. *Come on. Come on.*

Still no coverage. At least he'd fired off a text to the ranch foreman, Hawk, before tearing out of his house. He'd managed to coax Lady into the backseat, not wanting to leave her alone on her first night in a new house.

All it had taken was a little bit of bacon to get her up and moving after all the fluids she'd been given. The vitamins had helped and she had been given power food high in vitamins in as few bites as possible. It would take a little time for her stomach to stretch. But Hayden had a plan for that too.

When it came to rehabbing dogs, this wasn't his first rodeo so to speak. If only he was so experienced with women he was attracted to. The string of relationships—if they could be called that—since LeAnne had been nothing more than two people enjoying great sex with no strings attached. He was honest from the get-go. And his lovers accepted his terms. He liked to think they were cut from the same cloth as him, except that a couple had shown signs of wanting to stick around and make it a little more permanent.

The signs were easy to pick up on. 'Accidentally' leaving behind a favorite shirt or even a toothbrush. Hayden had a strict rule about no sleepovers, and a couple of his cohorts had tried to violate the restriction. Sleepovers got too confusing. Were they in a real relationship? Were they just hooking up for mutual pleasure? Lines were blurred when pajamas were involved. His no pajamas rule had been teased by at least two offering to sleep naked.

Waking up to someone? That was a huge step in a relationship. One he just couldn't seem to get himself to with anyone since LeAnne.

He kissed the band before tucking it inside his button-down shirt. He'd put on something besides a T-shirt. Miss Penny would be proud. His usual pair of jeans sufficed. Getting ready, thinking about what to wear...those didn't generally cause him to work up a sweat in the way tonight had. For reasons he didn't want to examine, he cared a lot about what Mika thought of his appearance.

Using voice recognition, he asked his phone to call her again. This time, it rang and then went straight into voice-mail. So, naturally, his imagination snapped into overdrive.

A beautiful woman stranded on a farm road that wasn't exactly on the beaten path. Okay, he couldn't let himself go there. He couldn't go to the place where she was lying on the side of the road or not there at all, abducted.

Again, he called. Again, he got voicemail. Again, he smacked the steering wheel with the flat of his palm.

The thought of anything bad happening to her lanced his chest.

8

uddenly Hayden's cell rang. Using voice commands,
he answered, and the sweetest voice came through
his truck speakers...Mika.

"Are you okay?" he asked. His heart jackhammering his
ribs as he waited for a response.

"Yes. I think. There's no blood. Nothing's broken. This is
probably going to sound stupid but I've had a few cases at
work that have thrown me off balance. It feels like someone
is watching me and I've had the sensation before. A couple
of times actually."

"When?"

"Today at Lady's house. In the woods when I was
chasing her. At my house earlier. The truth is that I couldn't
wait to get out of there," she admitted, making an effort to
mask her fears. He picked up on a slight tremor in her voice
here and there but mostly she spoke calmly, like she was
reading ingredients off a cereal box. Most people would be
freaking out about now with one of those things happening
let alone all three. And, no, he didn't think she was crazy or
losing her mind. She was obviously going through a lot with

her family's situation and now he heard about the work threats. Those would throw anyone off their game.

"Tell me what's happening now," he said.

"It's probably nothing." Those three words caused him to sit up a little straighter.

"Just in case it's not. What do you see?"

"I heard something in the underbrush when I was talking to you before. We got cut off and I could have sworn I saw movement. It's probably just this deer's family." Her voice trembled ever so slightly on the last part. "But either way, it stressed me out. I jumped inside my car and locked the doors. I'm being paranoid, right?"

"I hope that's all it is. You're right to stay inside the car, though. Locking the doors is just good sense. I've always gotten by on gut instinct. If yours told you something was off, it probably was. Besides, there's nothing wrong with waiting in your car or playing it safe."

"Really? Because I feel like I'm starting to lose it."

"You're fine. Believe me." A text came in that Hawk had received the message and was on his way. He was about fifteen minutes behind Hayden. The ranch foreman could take care of Mika's vehicle and get the deer to the side of the road so no one accidentally hit it a second time. Country roads weren't well lit and someone—although not too many people were on this particular stretch—could have an accident.

He kept her on the line for the rest of the drive, flashing his headlights when he got close to where he figured she'd be. "Do you see me?"

"Yes." The relief in her voice was palpable.

"Hold tight. The cavalry is about to arrive behind me."

"As far as I'm concerned, it's already here," she said low and under her breath. The words, her voice, traveled through him, cracking a piece of his armor as it zeroed in on its target. She brought a peek of light into the darkest place —places he believed no one would ever reach again. Rather than read too much into the situation, he, for once, just went with it.

He turned on his emergency flashers on the off chance anyone else drove down the road. He didn't want to catch anyone off guard. He turned to Lady, who looked mighty comfortable on the blanket in the backseat. "Wait here, girl. I'll be right back."

Leaving the engine on idle, he hopped out of the truck and made a beeline for the sedan that was jacked up on the side of the road. Her headlights lit the opposite side of the road and it looked like she was wedged pretty good inside a ditch. The front of her vehicle was banged up. The door opened and when Mika stepped out, Hayden's heart faltered. She had on a white lacy minidress that showed off her tanned legs. Her feet were tucked inside tan and teal boots, and she had on a faded denim jacket along with a turquoise necklace and earrings. He didn't normally notice earrings, but on her, he noticed.

He also noticed the way the breeze toyed with her hair as she took a step toward him and how alive his senses became any time she was near. The breeze carried a lightly floral scent, a mix of spring flowers and citrus.

In fact, Hayden stalked right toward her. When he got close enough to reach out and touch her, she locked gazes with him and his heart took another hit.

"Are you married, Hayden McGannon?" Her words came out like an accusation.

"Not anymore." He brought his right hand up to cup her cheek. He slid his fingers through her hair and brought those pink lips of hers closer to his. The second her lips pressed against his, fireworks shot off inside him. Electricity pulsed, heating his skin and causing his breath to come out in rasps.

Thank the heavens she seemed to be having the same reaction to the kiss as she closed her eyes and brought her hands up to his shoulders. For a split second, he expected her to push him away. Instead, her fingertips dug into his skin through the thin material of his shirt.

She pulled back long enough to say, "You look nice."

He laughed against her lips before claiming them again. A few seconds later, he managed to say against her lips, "You're beautiful."

And then he claimed her mouth with bruising need. Hot and heavy didn't begin to describe the moment as he slipped his free hand around her waist and hauled her against his chest. Her body, flush with his, sent rockets of desire shooting through him. More of that heat seeking an outlet flooded him. Flames boiled his blood.

He'd never gotten so worked up in such a short time before. Her full pink lips were soft against his. She parted them for him and he dipped his tongue inside where she tasted like a mix of peppermint and honey. His favorite new flavor mix.

With her body pressed to his and his tongue inside her mouth, it was easy to let the rest of the world slip away. But then Lady barked.

"Hold that thought," he said to Mika, linking their fingers as they made a beeline for the truck.

A look inside revealed that she was sleeping. A nightmare?

Hayden didn't want to startle her, so he opened the driver's side door. He tapped the dome light button so it would turn off.

"You're okay," he soothed.

She started running in her sleep. On her side, her paws were working double time. He didn't want her to wear out what little energy she had gained.

"Lady," he said a little bit louder. "You're all right."

Mika tapped him on the shoulder. "Mind if I try?"

"Be my guest." He stepped aside to allow her room to climb into the seat facing the back. Hayden had to force his gaze away from her backside.

"Hey, sweet girl. Lady," she practically cooed.

Lady's head went up and her gaze locked onto Mika. Her tail gave a quick wag before her head went back on the seat and she relaxed.

"How'd you do that?" He wasn't used to someone teaching him a thing or two about animals.

"I suspected that she might respond to a female voice a little bit better right now. The neighbor who has been sneaking her food and water is a woman. Her owner is a male. She might have a negative association with men because of his neglect," she pointed out. "It'll take time but she'll get over it. She needs you more than you realize."

Before Hayden could respond or claim those full pink lips again, headlights cut through the darkness.

"How many trucks are coming?" Her eyes widened when she caught sight of the cavalry.

"Looks like just two."

"Just?" She blinked at him.

He couldn't help himself. He dipped his head and kissed her one more time. These shouldn't rank up there as the best kisses he'd ever experienced, considering he'd been married. But there'd been special circumstances there.

And he'd been waiting a long time for someone like

Mika to come along. Too bad the relationship couldn't go anywhere.

MIKA NEEDED a minute to catch her breath. She couldn't think straight while Hayden's thick, gorgeous lips were pressed to hers. The man could kiss. There was so much heat they could start a wildfire during a spring thunderstorm.

She should probably ask for a ride back to her house where she could make a few calls to insurance and a rental car company. But when his arms had been around her and she was pressed against that silk over steel body of his, all reason flew out the window.

Both trucks pulled up behind Hayden's vehicle.

"Mind if I stay here with her?" Mika asked, motioning toward Lady.

"No. In fact, I was about to suggest it."

She climbed inside the driver's seat as he headed back to greet the cavalry. In her mind, Hayden was the cavalry.

Maybe she needed more than three days off the job. The threats were starting to get to her. Granted, there'd been something extra prickly about O'Rourke's, considering his connections. Then there was the super-spoiled, used to getting his way athlete known for his selfish behavior and antics on and off the field, Jimenez, didn't sit right.

It could have been the fact the threats had come back-to-back, and at a time when she was down because of her family situation, that had her blowing their words out of proportion. It would be nice if her sister lived closer. There was no chance Mel was moving back to Texas. She loved Colorado and her husband's job was there. Besides, with three young kids, it wasn't practical to think her sister would be able to pitch in very much when it came to their mother. If anything, Mel would move closer to home to get help, not give it.

Mika didn't want to resent her sister for having a family and being too busy to pitch in. She was just thinking it would be nice to share the responsibility with someone else. Depending on the settlement her mother got in the divorce, Mika might be able to hire someone to fill in the gaps while she was at work. Mika's job was what she considered a heart job. Emotionally fulfilling but definitely not a money maker.

Mel had already made it clear she was strapped for cash. Her offer was to take their mother for a week now and then she'd see how it goes to take her another week in a couple of months. They both knew travel would be short-lived for their mother once she progressed. But the timeline for that was a great unknown.

Catching sight of Hayden in the rearview mirror, Mika vowed to set those heavy thoughts aside.

Hayden stopped with two men, one older and one younger, at his side. "Mika, I'd like to introduce you to the man who keeps, and has kept, the ranch running smoothly for decades. We call him Hawk and he's part of our family."

"It's a pleasure to meet you." She smiled and an emotion stirred behind Hayden's eyes that she couldn't quite identify. Pride?

"The pleasure is all mine," Hawk beamed. The introduction no doubt touched his heart.

"This young man is Trevor, and he's an invaluable member of the team," Hayden said, tipping his hat toward the younger man who immediately stepped forward.

"Nice to meet you, Trevor."

"Ma'am." He tipped his hat in show of respect. She

would never get tired of southern charm or southern manners. To be fair, Texas was southwestern and that was different from a place like Georgia. But there were similarities in mannerisms and being a gentleman was one of them.

"We'll get you fixed right up," Hawk said. "And we'll make sure a needy family gets the meat from the deer so it doesn't go to waste."

"That would be amazing. Thank you," she said, impressed with how well they'd thought it out.

Trevor followed Hawk to her car. He pulled a pair of work gloves out of his back pocket and put them on before getting to it. He and Trevor worked like a well-oiled machine. With Hayden pulling up a truck, they had her car hooked up and out of the ditch in a manner of minutes. The speed in which they worked was impressive. The deer was handled next, wrapped up and placed in the back of the second truck.

Within the span of fifteen minutes or so, the entire situation had been handled and Hayden was headed back toward the truck. Lady was sleeping in fits, no doubt a result of the trauma she'd experienced for the first three years of her life. Sweet girl.

Seeing him walk toward the truck, she picked up on a definite swagger in his gait that made him even more seductive. What was it about this man that was so different than everyone else she'd dated?

"We'll get your car fixed up ASAP," he began. "In the meantime, you're welcome to borrow one of the vehicles on the ranch."

She blinked a couple of times. Was this guy for real?

"What?" he asked with a raised eyebrow.

She must've made one heckuva face based on his reaction. She reached out and playfully pinched him on the forearm.

"What was that for?"

"Just checking to see if you're real or a figment of my imagination." She laughed. Loud. Like a full-belly laugh. And it was the first time since her mother's diagnosis that she'd really laughed.

That raised eyebrow of his made her laugh even more.

"Sorry." She managed to stop laughing long enough to get out the word. "I'm seriously losing it. I know. Don't take this the wrong way. But for a minute, I thought there was no way you could exist."

"I'm going to take that as a compliment." He studied her like he was trying to figure out if she'd lost her marbles.

"It is. You should," she said quickly. "I mean, first, you kissed me in a way that I've seriously never been kissed before. Ever. And now you're digging my car out of a ditch while offering a replacement. And we just met this morning. Who trusts people that much?"

"This might surprise you to know but the ranching community has survived weather, disease, and drought, all by depending on each other. We don't take our community responsibilities lightly and we help anyone who needs it. Not because we're saints. Believe me, we're not. But because it's ingrained in us and it's part of the reason ranching is more than a job. It's who I am."

The slight defensiveness to his tone made her rethink her outburst.

"I'm sorry. I didn't mean any of that as an insult. And I haven't really laughed in too long. I'm basically loopy at this point. It's been a long day and I should be asking you to take me home right now because of it. But I don't want to go home." She paused right there, hoping she hadn't said too much.

She risked a glance at him to see his face muscles had relaxed and a smile had crept across those thick lips of his.

"Did you say the best kiss you've ever had?" He broke into a wide smile now.

"Take me to your house?" She wasn't answering his question. No way. A warm blush had already crawled up her neck, giving away the effect he had on her.

He took off his gloves, tossed them in the back, and practically bathed in hand sanitizer before returning to the driver's seat. She scooted over to the middle seat.

After claiming the driver's seat, he leaned over and pressed the sweetest, most gentle kiss to her lips. A dozen butterflies took flight in her stomach, and she was just beginning to realize how much trouble she was in with this man.

9

Hayden opened the door for Mika as Lady tailed behind. He had to admit the dog seemed more comfortable with Mika than she did with him. Her point about a male being the one to inflict pain on the sweet animal was probably dead on.

Lady needed to know that all men weren't bad. He had every confidence she would warm up to him given enough time. And he planned to give her all the time she needed. He had no timetable for her healing. He would allow her to take the lead. The fact that she responded to Mika was a good sign that all humans weren't bad in her eyes. He could work with that.

"Your home is beautiful," Mika said after taking a couple of steps inside. "This whole property is beyond anything I've ever seen before."

"Don't be too impressed. We're all pretty normal people who have been fortunate." He wanted her to feel comfortable on the ranch for reasons that ran deeper than he wanted to delve into. At least for tonight, he didn't want to get inside his head about what anything meant. He wanted to be able to enjoy the moment without automatically pushing her away. Because the few kisses they'd shared had been right up there as the best for him too.

"There's nothing normal about you, Hayden McGannon." There was so much admiration in her voice that his heart clenched. "And I mean that in the best possible way."

He tucked a loose tendril of hair behind her ear. Temptation stared him in the eyes.

Her stomach growled, reminding him that he'd promised her a meal.

"Sorry. I haven't eaten since lunch."

He'd almost forgotten about the pizza from DOUGH. "I have food."

Wow, wasn't he crushing it with the words. That was about as caveman sounding as it got. Me. Food. You. Eat. Would have been on par with what had just come out of his mouth.

Hayden cracked a smile. No one had had the same effect on him. Not even...

He stopped himself right there before he ruined the evening by getting inside his head. He didn't want to go there. Not tonight. Tonight, he would give it a rest.

"Follow me," he said with a smile.

"Food can wait a few minutes. I want a tour first." Her honey-brown eyes were wide as she took in the two-story fireplace.

"This is the family room." He walked her into the two-story space and then turned around to face her. Seeing his home through her eyes made it feel brand new.

"I don't think I've ever seen a more beautiful fireplace." She walked over and smoothed her hand along the stacked layers of stones and his chest swelled with something that felt a whole lot like pride.

"The star over the mantle is gorgeous."

"A friend of the family made it. Samuel Johnson."

"*The* Samuel Johnson?" It was easy to forget how well known Samuel had become for his bronzes.

"One and the same. It was a housewarming gift."

"I'm impressed," she admitted. "And you no longer get to give the everyday-man-spiel. This is special."

No, *she* was special. But he did appreciate the gift from a friend and the work of art for its beauty.

He cleared his throat.

"The couches look like the kind I could just sink into," she said, without missing a beat. Twin tan-colored couches faced each other. A hand-carved oak coffee table sat in between. Each had a sofa table behind it with a small bronze, books, and lamps. She walked over and picked up a novel. "And they say people don't read anymore."

"Miss Penny wouldn't have had it any other way." He smiled at the memories. "She sat us down every night when we were little and read a book to us. Each took a turn picking one out from a selection. She read a lot of Louis L'Amour to us, and the habit stuck with me and my brothers." Strange that he'd just referred to his cousins as brothers too. It was the way things used to be before life got so complicated and the family became divided.

"She sounds like a wonderful person." Those words, the kindness in them, warmed his heart.

"She is. I'd like the two of you to meet someday." He spoke before he had time to filter his thoughts. He wasn't trying to jump ahead of the game here.

Mika didn't answer, she just continued to take in the room. Her gaze stopped on the small picture frame next to the stack of books.

LeAnne in her wedding dress. No matter how much time had passed, he couldn't seem to toss it out.

Mika paused in front of the picture, running her finger along the delicate frame. She kept her gaze lowered, her eyes hooded with those thick black lashes of hers. She had to have questions. Any reasonable person would.

He braced himself, ready for them.

Lady walked beside Mika, and then off to the bed he'd made for her out of his thickest and softest blankets. She took her spot next to the fireplace and then curled up in a ball.

"She sure is making herself comfortable," Mika said.

"Yep." He waited for the other questions—the ones about his wife and why he wasn't still married.

Mika hesitated for a long moment in front of the frame before moving into the adjacent dining room. The open-concept space made it easy to keep an eye on Lady while she rested as they moved into the next room.

"Hand-carved?" She pointed to the dining table with room for ten.

"Yes."

"Same person as the coffee table?" she asked. He was impressed she'd noticed.

"Yes."

"This place is a dream, Hayden. It's surprisingly...masculine."

Did she think his wife had lived here? Decorated the place? It probably wasn't an assumption that was too far off base.

"I decorated it myself. With the help of Aunt Penny," he clarified.

"Oh, really?" Her shock confirmed his suspicion.

"I've lived here for about five years now. It's all relatively new," he said, deciding against telling her that he'd lived in the main house with his wife while this one was being built. Then he couldn't bring himself to move in, so it sat empty for a good many years.

He started to reach for the necklace but clenched his fist instead and rested it on the back of a dining chair. "The kitchen was mostly Miss Penny. I already told you that I wasn't much of a cook. I'm great at reheating, though."

Needing to keep moving, he walked into the next room. "She figured out how many cabinets I would need and where."

"I've never built a house from scratch. The sheer number of decisions that would have to be made would throw me in a tailspin. I'm good with walking into a structure and figuring out what to do with it. But, not from the studs. I need an outline to work with," she said. The smile was gone from her eyes and he knew the reason.

There were too many questions rolling around in her head about his past, about his marriage. As much as he didn't want to talk about LeAnne—he never did with anyone—he figured Mika needed to know something or she'd never relax.

"She died." He walked over to the picture frame and then picked it up. "My wife. We were just kids."

"OH, Hayden. I'm so sorry. That's such a horrible thing to go through." Mika slid onto the barstool that was pushed up to the granite island. "You don't have to talk about it if—"

He shook his head. "I've never wanted to talk about it with anyone until you. But I also promised to feed you, so can we talk whilst we eat?"

"Yes. That sounds like a plan." She wanted to be a friend to Hayden. If she was being totally honest, she wanted to be a whole lot more than that, but she'd settle for friendship. And since she was facing reality, she could use a friend in return. She had a lot of contacts through work. She was friendly with many of the kind people she met and even stayed in touch, exchanging the occasional holiday card with some. Every year, the front of her fridge ended up covered in pet photos with Santa. She loved those and it brought joy to her heart to see all those happy stories.

Hayden started pulling containers out of the fridge.

"What can I do to help?" She pushed up to standing and came around the island.

"Sit."

"No chance, I intend to earn my keep. Now, show me where you keep the plates or I'll just start randomly opening cabinets," she warned.

His chuckle was a rumble from deep in his chest. "We can't have you opening things. That would mess up the natural order." He pointed to the cabinet to the right of the sink. "Glasses are in there. What will you have to drink?"

"Do you have ice tea?"

"Do we live in Texas?" He winked and more of those butterflies released. "The question isn't whether or not we have tea, it's how do you take it?"

"This isn't very southern of me but I like my tea the same way I take my coffee, straight up," she said, grabbing a pair of glasses.

"Then, pour two glasses. Pitcher is in the fridge. Miss Penny keeps us stocked with just about everything we could want. We consume it because we were taught not to waste."

Mika set the glasses down on the counter before walking over and opening the fridge door. "Holy smokes. Think Miss

Penny would be willing to swing by my house for like a week? My fridge has mostly takeout boxes in it and has never been this full."

Hayden laughed and it was about the best sound she'd ever heard. His masculine tone sent a sensual shiver racing across her skin, goosebumping her arms.

She poured the tea, very aware of his male presence as he passed behind her with two plates of food. One by one, they went into the microwave and the house was filled with the most amazing smell.

"Where are we eating, by the way?" She motioned toward the granite island.

He nodded toward the dinner table.

"Nice," she said under her breath.

"Agreed," he responded.

Her cheeks flamed, so she ducked her head, chin to chest, trying to hide her embarrassment. She shouldn't be embarrassed. She hadn't done anything to embarrass herself. Just being around Hayden caused her body to warm and her blush to crawl up her neck. So, she wasn't doing a great job at hiding the whole attraction thing. This generally wasn't a problem for her. But then, she hadn't been around too many men like him.

"I think everything is ready," he said. When he looked at her, her knees weakened. The earlier scare of her feeling like she was being watched had been confirmed as just that —her imagination getting the best of her.

She joined him at the table for a meal of the best smelling, best looking plate of spaghetti and meatballs she could remember. "My mouth is watering just standing here."

"Then sit down and eat."

She did. All it took was one bite for her to mewl with

pleasure.

He cocked a smile and cleared his throat, but didn't say a word.

Curiosity was getting the better of her about his wife. She sized him up to be around thirty years old, give or take. Same as her. Wow, had she really hit thirty already? Yes, she mused. Last year. How had the time gotten away from her and how had she not remembered such a landmark birthday?

Work. She'd been working long hours trying to place a shepherd mix that was afraid of his own shadow. The week had been especially busy between him and the half dozen feral kittens that needed foster homes. Finding a good dog or cat a home around the holidays was easy. Placing one in foster care? Not so much.

"I promised you that I'd tell you my story. I'll make it quick because I honestly would rather spend tonight getting to know you." The sincerity in Hayden's words sent more of that warmth spiraling through her.

She took a deep breath and then set her fork down.

"No. Keep eating. I promised you food and I know you're starved," he said.

She picked up the fork and toyed with the spaghetti.

"LeAnne was my high school sweetheart. We were on and off since we were fifteen. Probably better off as friends but we loved each other and we confused it for something romantic. We broke up half a dozen times trying to figure it all out. Probably hurt each other more than anything else. We ended up convincing ourselves that we could live without each other after she moved to Austin for college. She came home, and then dropped out of school. I asked her to marry me. She said yes. We got married at her parent's place and moved into the main house while cooking up plans for this place. I lost her before construction was finished."

Mika reached across the table and touched Hayden's hand. "That must have been awful for you. I'm so sorry."

"Thank you." The sincerity in his words touched her. The stress lines across his forehead relaxed a little bit and it was almost like he exhaled. Then, he cocked a smile. "That's enough talk about the past."

Was it, though? There was a picture of his wife in his living room and he wore his wedding band around his neck. Mika realized he never got over the woman and there was no way she could compete with a ghost. Not that she was trying to. But memories were powerful.

Still, she was honored that he shared his story with her after saying he didn't talk about it with anyone.

"I can see that I've killed the mood now," he said.

"Actually, I was just about to thank you for opening up to me," she countered. "I'm honored that you trust me enough to talk about your past."

Her words, pale as they might be considering what he'd just shared, seemed to appease him.

"Tell me why you got into the animal rescue business." He changed the subject and she could sense that the other topic was put to rest for the night. Maybe for the rest of their friendship. And she hoped this was the beginning of something and not a temporary stop. Although, with her mother's condition, Mika couldn't see having a whole lot of time for much other than work.

"I grew up in a small suburb of Houston where I used to babysit to make extra money. There was this dog that I loved at one of the houses. She was the sweetest thing. My dad nixed the idea of us getting a dog of our own, so I considered all the pets on my babysitting circuit mine too."

Suddenly, the tines of her fork became very interesting. She studied them. "So, Bella technically belonged to the mother. She was the cutest thing and would sit on my lap long after the kids went to sleep. I would stroke her fur while doing my homework or watching TV. Anyway, turns out the mom was having an affair and to punish her, the father...let's just say he took out his frustrations on her dog. This couple fought all the time in front of me. He kicked Bella once. I should have done something but I didn't know who to call."

"The man should be castrated," Hayden said with conviction.

"Agreed." Today, she would handle the situation so differently. "The whole incident left an impression on me and I wanted to find a job where I could speak up for innocent animals because they have no voice."

"No wonder she loves you so much." He motioned toward Lady, who was resting peacefully.

"I always thought dogs could see into your heart. You know? Of course, now that I've been working with them for many years, I realize some are more attuned to people than others. But someone has to be their voice," she said wistfully.

This was an evening of firsts. Because Hayden was the first person she'd told the real reason she'd ditched college in favor of working to benefit animals.

"They're lucky to have someone like you looking out for them," he said with admiration.

This was also the first time she'd been drawn to someone in a very long time. She'd dated around. She'd had a couple of semi-serious relationships. She'd had her fair share of first dates.

But being with Hayden felt so right and so dangerous—dangerous to her heart.

10

Hayden was in trouble.

Talking to Mika was the first he'd mentioned LeAnne to someone without the last name McGannon. He rarely talked about her with his brothers or his cousins. He was still surprised in the fact that he'd *wanted* Mika to know about her. Granted, he'd kept a few important pieces of information to himself. No one needed to know the whole truth. What would it change? Nothing. What would it do? Nothing. What would it gain? Nothing.

"Coffee?" he asked, not quite wanting the night to end after dinner.

"Yes, please. But you have to let me do the dishes at least," she said.

"I'm not going to argue that offer."

She cracked a smile and his chest filled with pride for lightening her mood.

"I'm sorry about earlier on the phone back on the road when I was freaking out about someone watching me. Clearly, I was wrong about it."

"Don't be. You never know what is out in the woods. An

animal could have been stalking the deer and then set its sights on you."

"I hadn't really thought about the possibility. Makes perfect sense, though."

"Deer are blinded by headlights, so the animal might have been gunning to get away from a coyote or black bear," he said.

"The thought of eyes on me instead gives me a case of the willies." She visibly shuttered.

"It's why I suggested that you wait inside your car." He winked. "Wanted to keep you safe so you could keep taking care of all the other animals."

"Even if there was an animal out there. I've been jumpy lately. Had a couple cases at work that I just can't shake."

"Did someone threaten you?" His blood pressure shot up and his protective instincts flared.

"Oh, I get threats all the time." She blew out a breath. "Normally, I don't take it seriously. Despite these people being the lowest scum for abusing animals, in their mind I'm taking away something they think belongs to them."

"That's their first problem. We don't own nature." He shook his head.

"I'm always saying the same thing. This is a life. We don't 'own' a being."

"What got you about these cases?" he asked.

She started to respond when Lady stretched before standing up. She walked over to her water bowl, which was basically a serving bowl that he'd put up on a stool so she wouldn't have to bend down too far to reach her water. Her food bowl was still full from earlier. Derek had sent him home with enough supplies to get through a few days without needing to make a run to the store. Although, there was always enough food in the barn given the sheer number of animals on the property.

She moved to the food bowl and took a couple of bites.

Mika's gaze bounced from Lady to Hayden and back. The pure smile on her face brought light to more of his darkest places. She practically beamed and he was grateful the mood shifted. They'd talked about some heavy topics earlier. Part of his burden had been lifted. It was strange because he didn't even realize how much he'd been holding inside until he talked about Leanne with Mika. There was a lightness to his step that he hadn't felt in years. He wanted more.

"I can't believe she's eating on her own already," she said.

"She's doing better on all fronts now that you're here." He meant it.

He was rewarded with a smile that caused his heart to clench as he handed over a cup of fresh coffee.

"That literally took, like, two seconds to make. How on earth...?" she asked.

"I don't mess around when it comes to my coffee. This machine is one of the very few investments I've made. It stocks these pods at the perfect temperature. The thing is plumbed, so all I have to do is push a button and make sure there's a cup underneath there to catch the stream."

"I watched and yet I still don't believe this is possible. Mankind has finally perfected something worthwhile," she teased as she took a sip. "And this coffee is to die for."

"It's good."

"Hey," she started and then bit her lip like she was stopping herself from an impulse.

"What?"

"Do you want to drink these outside once Lady's finished eating?" Standing there in his kitchen was the most beautiful woman. If she wanted to drink coffee outside, they were drinking coffee outside. "Sounds like a plan to me. I never turn down a chance to get out of a building."

Mika leaned her hip against the counter as she took another sip and he couldn't help but think how right she looked standing in his kitchen.

Lady glanced up at him.

"Do you want to go outside?" he asked, more to train her what was coming next after she heard those words.

"Did she just wag her tail?" Mika asked.

"Hey, look at that. Progress." It was the first time Lady gave any hint she was anything but scared of him. It was most likely because Mika was in the room, but he'd take it.

Capitalizing on the moment, he walked to the back door and then held it open for Mika. She walked out with Lady on her heels. Hayden forced his gaze away from Mika's backside. He issued a sharp sigh before following them out the door. He grabbed a treat for Lady for after she did her business. Anything with bacon flavoring was usually a powerful motivator.

She went right out to the yard and took care of things. She walked over next to a tree and stood. His heart took a hit.

"Not anymore, girl. You belong with us now," he said, walking over to her and coaxing her onto the back porch with a treat.

"Would you look at that sky," Mika said, taking a seat on the outdoor sofa.

"There isn't much more beautiful than Texas at night," he agreed. "Present company excluded."

"I don't know about that. Look at those stars. They're so bright. I never got to see this many growing up near Houston."

"Light pollution. That's the problem with a major city."
He paused. "Or should I say that's just one of many problems with living in a major city."

"You never had a desire to live anywhere else?" she
asked.

"Never. This ranch, this land is as much part of me as
being a McGannon."

She looked around at the land. She glanced back at the
house. "This place is truly magical. If I grew up here, I'd
never want to leave either."

"We have everything we could ever need right here," he
admitted, wanting to add the words, especially now, but
didn't.

It was a good sign that he was willing to open up and
talk to someone about his past. Maybe it was time to start
letting that piece of him go. He'd never stop loving LeAnne.
She'd been special and what they'd had together could
never be replaced. He didn't even want to think about trying.
Had Coby hit on a point when he'd said Hayden should
loosen up a little bit? Maybe make a little room for someone
else in his life. It didn't have to be the woman sitting next to
him. Although, he reached his hand out and clasped hers
without thinking too much about it.

The familiar jolt of electricity pulsed through his fingertips and a word came to mind, *home*.

"What do you think about staying the night?" he asked.

MIKA WAS CAUGHT off guard by the question. She should
say *no thanks*. She should go home and maybe check out
some of the paperwork waiting there. To be honest, she
wasn't going to. The drive was long and in a borrowed

vehicle. By the time she got home she'd flop in bed anyway.

Plus, she didn't *want* to go home. She wanted to stay right here. No funny business involved.

"Is the guest room made up?" She wanted to make her intentions clear.

"It is."

"Does Miss Penny always have it ready to go?" she asked out of sheer curiosity.

"She does. Fresh linens on the bed and towels in the guest bath," he admitted on a laugh. "I rarely ever have company and never overnight. She knows this but insists a guest room should be ready to go at all times. Guess I should thank her if that's the reason you're about to agree to staying over."

"I haven't agreed to staying overnight yet," she quipped, unable to hide her smirk. He'd pegged her, not that it was difficult. This one time, she wished she could be a one-night-stand girl. One night of absolute ecstasy sounded exactly what she needed right now. But, no. She needed at least the thought of a commitment before she could go there with anyone, including the man who was temptation on a stick.

"But you will." The Cheshire cat grin on his face would be infuriating if it wasn't so stinking sexy.

"In the guest room."

"You'd know if I was inviting you to my bed." Didn't those words send a sensual shiver skittering across her skin?

"Oh yeah?" She did her best to play it cool. "I wouldn't count on that any time soon, cowboy."

"Shame," was all he said.

The two of them just sat there. She couldn't be certain for how long. The only sounds were the chorus of cicadas and grasshoppers. The occasional lightning bug lit up across the yard. She'd loved those when she was a kid. She was the only kid on the block who didn't have the heart to put them in a jar and keep them inside.

She took a sip of coffee, thinking this night couldn't be more perfect. She could breathe out here. It probably didn't hurt that she felt more than protected between Hayden and Lady. Plus, security getting onto the ranch was tight. Out on the land, she knew there were poachers. She didn't think they'd come this close to the residences, though.

So, it was just her, Hayden, and Lady, under a blanket of stars on a night sky that was as clear as she'd ever seen and seemed to go on forever.

"I could stay out here all night," she admitted.

"There have been plenty of nights tracking poachers that I've spent under this sky. Never gets old," he said.

"I kind of wish we'd..." She didn't have the heart to finish her sentence.

"Met under different circumstances?" he asked.

"Yes. Strange. How did you know what I was thinking?"

"Because I just had the same thought." He brought her hand up to his lips and pressed the most tender kiss on the back of her hand. Her stomach free fell as though she were base jumping.

Complicated didn't begin to describe this period in her life and, based on what he'd told her earlier, he had demons. There was no way she could compete with a ghost.

Since there was no use trying and they had tonight to spend together, she decided this would be enough. Sitting out here, with him and Lady, was the best date she'd had in longer than she could remember. Despite the electricity pinging between them, the draw to him was undeniable.

And, for tonight, she wanted to enjoy this night for all it

was worth because this memory was going to have to get her through the months to come and remind her of how good life could be.

The next thing she knew, Hayden released her hand. He looped his arm around her shoulders, and then she settled into the crook of his arm. The electrical current running between them intensified and her skin quivered where it made contact with his.

She could bask in the glow of the full moon lighting a perfect night sky forever. The cold front that had threatened never materialized. That was the thing about Texas weather. Stick around for five minutes and it would change, as the saying went. She could attest to the truth there. In case the front was moving in overnight, she should get up and check the weather on her phone.

Mika hadn't slept over anyone's house in a year. Not since her last boyfriend. The relationship had gone longer than most, five months. She'd spent exactly three nights at his place. Pete had been a beat cop in Houston. They'd met at a fundraiser; she'd been there for work and he'd been hired as security, but basically that meant he was a glorified parking attendant. Pete was a good guy right up until she realized he was still going through a divorce. He'd specifically said *divorced,* not separated.

When she'd called him out on the lie, he'd asked what the difference was. He was no longer living with his wife. They were in the process of a divorce.

It had mattered to her, especially when she found out a month later the two had reconciled. At that point, all Mika could do was wish his wife good luck. For a man who upheld the letter of the law, he sure saw a lot of gray areas when he spoke about his marriage.

Mika never would have gone out with a married man.

She'd blamed herself and felt shame, despite the fact she had no idea his true relationship status. Getting over him had been the easy part. Letting herself off the hook? Not so much. Looking back, she'd probably been too hard on herself.

"Hey," Hayden's voice was low and gravelly...sexy.

She didn't realize she'd closed her eyes while she'd been lost in thought. She blinked them open, turned her head and reached up until her lips met his. He still had the taste of dark coffee on his tongue when he dipped it inside her mouth.

She moaned against his lips as he intensified the kiss. He removed the coffee cup from her hands, placed them on the table. She twisted toward him for better access. He brought his hands up to cup her face and his gaze locked onto hers.

"Do you have any idea how beautiful you are?" His words sent rockets of desire shooting through her. Warmth pooled low in her belly and heated the insides of her thighs.

"I could say the same thing to you," she shot back.

That got him to smile. She liked his smile. She liked being the one to make him smile. Because there was too much sadness behind those gorgeous brown eyes.

11

Hayden couldn't think of a better night.

Mika shivered against the breeze that had gotten cooler in the past five minutes. He had no idea how long they'd been there, kissing, but nothing in him wanted this night to be over.

"Are you cold?" He sized her up.

"No." Did she want to stay outside on his back porch as much as he did?

"Your lips are turning blue," he mused. "If we stay out here any longer your teeth are going to start chattering."

"Fine. Let's go inside."

"There's a fireplace to keep you warm." His comment elicited a smile that caused his heart to clench.

"Sold," she said, pushing up to standing. "Last one inside starts the fire."

With that, she bolted toward the door. There was one problem with her plan and it was the reason she wasn't gaining any forward momentum. He gripped her hips. Big mistake on his part. He didn't need to get used to the feel of those sweet round hips imprinting on his hands. His fingers involuntarily flexed and he could feel the electricity coursing through her.

He let go.

She darted for the door. He sat on his porch for a long moment, quirked a smile, and then followed after picking up the coffee cups. He stopped at the door she held open for him, and turned to look at Lady.

She didn't budge.

"Come on, girl," he said.

Her ears perked up but she lay there otherwise motionless.

"You're coming with me," he coaxed. "Come on."

For a minute there, he thought he was going to have to go inside for a treat. But she seemed to catch on. She jumped to her feet and moved toward him. Head down, her eyes on the ground, he encouraged her to keep coming toward him.

She stopped at the door and looked up.

Hayden made kissing noises as he entered the kitchen. She hesitated before following. But then she did follow. Her steps were tentative.

"That's right," he soothed. "One step at a time."

The sentiment hit him square in the chest. Ignoring it, he coaxed Lady into the kitchen.

"Good girl." He set the cups on the counter and then patted her on the head. "Progress."

Mika beamed at him before dropping down to Lady's level and giving her a good ear scratch. She said a few words meant to soothe the dog as he rinsed out the cups and then built a fire in the fireplace. He liked wood burning. He liked the heat. He liked the crackle sound the dried wood made when it burned.

"How's that for a fire?" It raged within a few minutes.

"Looks warm to me." Mika joined him in the living room. A phone's ringtone sounded, and a panicked look crossed her features. His mind immediately snapped to something happening with her mother.

She made a beeline for her purse, and then dug around for the device. She came up with it and immediately checked the screen. "It's my sister. I should take this."

"Go ahead." Hayden motioned toward the sofa as he moved into the kitchen. He fixed a second cup of coffee for both of them.

"Hey, what's going on?" Mika was quiet and he intentionally tried not to eavesdrop. It was difficult being in the same space despite being in separate rooms. That was the thing about open-concept spaces. There wasn't a whole lot of privacy. Not normally a problem for him, considering he lived alone. "Is she okay?"

Hayden set the cups on the counter and moved into his bedroom to get an extra pillow for Lady. By the time he came out, Mika was off the phone. She sat on the couch, staring at the fire.

"It's none of my business, but is everything okay?" He tucked the pillow underneath his arm and then brought over the pair of coffee cups. He set them on the table before adding the pillow to Lady's bed. She'd followed him into the bedroom and now the living room. She looked up at him tentatively before climbing on the bed and making herself comfortable.

"It is. Kind of," her voice was distant.

He figured she needed a minute, so he claimed a seat on the opposite sofa and took a sip of coffee.

"You know. My sister just called to complain about our mother and how needy she is right now." She leaned forward and reached for the coffee cup. "Thank you for this, by the way."

"Welcome."

"And the thing is that I never call her to complain. I always figure she's busy with her husband and the kids. I don't want to interrupt her family time or drag her down."

"Understandable. To a point," he said.

"Exactly. To a point. I never realized how self-centered my sister is before. She knew how much I needed this time off and yet she called me to vent. She wanted to know what I was doing and if I could research a couple of things for her tomorrow. Normally, I wouldn't mind but she knows this is my time off. She has to know I've been one hundred percent in charge of all the decisions for Mom. And she never volunteers to pitch in. She acts like sending Mom to stay with her for a week is a huge burden and that I owe her big time for 'helping' out," she said. Her toe tapped on the base of the coffee table, the tempo picking up with every word.

"While you're looking out for everyone else, including all the animals, who looks out for you?" Despite any disagreement with his brothers or cousins, any one of them would be right by his side in a heartbeat if they thought he needed them. He could count on any one of them to drop whatever they were doing if he put out a call for help. The fact that he didn't was on him. He was also starting to realize that if he wanted the family to stop breaking apart and start healing, maybe he was going to have to be the one to put out that call.

"Now? No one. It used to be my mom. She looked out for both me and my sister. She's the one who needs us now and I have no plans to abandon her or treat this situation like a burden. It's not going to be easy to watch my mom decline. I realize that. And I'm realistic enough to admit taking care of her on my own will be a handful."

"The job might become more than you can handle on your own," he pointed out before quickly adding, "you're fully capable in my eyes, it's just that I'm assuming you'll have to leave her alone to go to work."

"That's the part that scares me."

"Are you in a position to hire help?" He wasn't trying to embarrass her. He wanted to be able to fully assess the situation to see opportunities to help. His family had a charity and this was just the sort of case they loved. Being able to pitch in and help someone in need, to make a difference in someone's life, never got old.

"A lot depends on the settlement my father is willing to give my mother. Right now, it isn't looking good and she doesn't have the money to fight him on it." She blew out a frustrated breath. "But, I don't want to talk about my family right now. I know things are messed up and it's probably going to get worse. I have three days off work and six days before Mom comes back. I want to be ready for her when she gets here and that means taking a few days to forget I even have a family. Does that make me a jerk?"

"No. It makes you human." Ideas were already starting to pop on how he might be able to help the family. Those could wait. For now, he wanted to spend time with this beautiful and caring woman who deserved so much better than what life was handing her.

MIKA BIT BACK A YAWN. She didn't want this night to end. But it was getting late, she'd had a day for the books, and that was after getting up before the sun. Being with Hayden was

the best distraction she could think of because despite a
momentary slip, even thinking about her mom's situation
was less stressful around him. "Thank you."

He quirked a brow.

"I don't just mean for dinner. I mean for the whole day.
You helped me find this girl." She remembered how easily
he'd dropped everything to go on the hunt with a stranger.
"And thank you for rescuing me from the ditch."

"That, technically, was my fault," he pointed out with a
devastating grin.

She must've shot him a look because he quickly added,
"You never would have landed in the ditch if you weren't
coming to see me."

"True." She smiled back. Giving him a compliment
wasn't going over well. He was pro-level at deflecting.

"Believe me when I say that I'm glad you're here," he
added.

"Me too, Hayden. I can't think of the last time I liked
being with someone this much." The admission caused her
pulse to race. Even more so when he joined her on the sofa
and kissed her so thoroughly she lost her train of thought.
She got lost. Lost in the feeling of his lips moving against
hers. Lost in the feeling of his skin against hers. Lost in the
fog that was Hayden.

He pulled back too abruptly for her liking, and then
took her hands in his, tugging her to standing.

"You're tired. You need sleep. I'm taking you to bed." He
smirked again when he heard how that sounded. "To your
bed."

He was right. She'd lost all willpower. Plus, she didn't
want to be away from him even if they were still under the
same roof.

"Okay," she relented, following him to the stairs.

The guest bedroom could more accurately be described as a guest suite. The room itself was double the size of hers at home. There was a sitting area next to a wall of windows. The bed was massive, taking up one whole wall and she needed a small set of stairs to reach the top. They'd been pushed up beside it. There was no way it was only a king-sized bed. Did beds come in larger sizes?

The four posters were more of the hand-carved wood from the same person who'd done the dining table and coffee table.

"This room is beautiful," she said. "If I stay here tonight, how will I ever go home?"

"Don't tempt me." His comment may have come out low and under his breath, but it had the effect of a wildfire on her.

She decided to let it go. She had tonight with him. Then, a couple of days to recoup and prepare for the road ahead. She was already feeling better about the future. Being with Hayden made the world seem like a brighter place.

"Make yourself at home. There are spares of just about everything you could imagine in the bathroom. Toothpaste, toothbrushes, robes," he said.

"Miss Penny?"

He nodded. "Use anything you want. Keep anything you need."

"Oh, I forgot my cell phone downstairs. Maybe I should go...you know what? Never mind. I'm leaving it down there. No interruptions tonight." She walked to the door of the adjacent bathroom that looked more like a spa than a guest bathroom. She zeroed in on the tub. "Calgon, take me away."

His eyebrows knitted together in confusion.

"It's an old commercial for bath bubbles. My mom used

to say it all the time after a busy week." She smiled at the memory, thinking how nice it was to remember a good time with her mother.

"I'll be downstairs if you need anything." He moved to the door in a couple of quick strides. He stopped, bringing his hands up to the doorjamb. It was impossible not to notice the muscle bulges in his arms. She had to block the image of those arms wrapped around her in that big bed behind her. A red blush crawled up her cheeks.

Sexual chemistry wasn't a problem when it came to this man. Mentally, she hadn't clicked with anyone so easily in... well...ever. So it was a shame she had to go back to her life tomorrow and leave him behind. But, what a night to remember him by.

"I was serious about the offer. Use whatever you want and let me know if there's anything that will make tonight more comfortable."

"Will do," was all she could say and she barely got that out for how quickly her throat was drying out being alone in the bedroom with Hayden.

It looked like he was about to say something else before he clamped his mouth shut, and then walked away.

Mika stood rooted to the spot for at least a minute. Temptation had just left the room. The room had been charged with so much electricity that once he left the air cooled. She would need a fan to take with her down to breakfast so she could fan herself.

Very funny, Mika.

With a lighter step, she moved into the bathroom, stopping at the entrance to marvel a little bit more. If this was the guest bath, she could only imagine what the master must look like. She glanced around, taking in the free-standing tub in front of a mosaic that looked like something out of the Sistine Chapel. There were candles everywhere she looked. The white robe hanging on the door looked like something out of a brochure for a five-star hotel. There was a round tufted ottoman in the middle of the room with the softest-looking rug underneath. The teal blue ottoman was made of some kind of velvet material.

Everything was understated rather than showy. This place matched its owner to a T.

While the bath filled with water, she located matches and then walked around lighting candles. When the last one was lit, she hit the dimmer switch on the chandelier that hung in the middle of the room.

Slipping out of her clothes and into the tub, the stress from earlier in the day melted away. There was a tray across the tub filled with scrubs and brushes that were still in wrappers. The soap smelled like a lavender field.

She could definitely get used to this treatment.

Her thoughts drifted to Hayden. How sad was it the woman he loved had died? From what she could tell, he hadn't gotten involved in a relationship since. The picture of his wife was young. Had they been out of their teens?

Young love didn't normally beat the odds, but Hayden knew his own mind. He was the rare type who probably did find the woman he loved and knew he was ready. He was the kind who would commit forever and actually follow through.

Her heart went out to him for losing someone so young and when they were so in love. She couldn't imagine getting over a heartbreak like that so early in life. No one could walk away from that unscathed. And even all these years later, he still wore his wedding ring around his neck.

She couldn't imagine having that kind of devotion. Her

sister was married but Mika couldn't say either one was dedicated to the other to that degree, and they had children.

Hayden was one of a kind. And a piece of her heart wanted him to be hers.

Tonight, she would hold onto the fairytale. Tomorrow, she would accept a reality check.

12

S leep wasn't normally a problem for Hayden, but that night he slept in fits and starts. So when his internal alarm woke him up at four a.m., he gave up on sleep, pushed off the covers and threw on a pair of jeans.

Coffee. He needed to clear his thoughts because all he'd thought about was the woman sleeping upstairs.

Lady was curled up in the corner of his room, looking like she was concerned she'd done something wrong by being in the house. She'd get used to her new life. The progress she'd made already was beyond anything he'd expected.

He patted her on the head before moving into his bathroom to splash cold water on his face and brush his teeth. There wasn't much worse than morning breath.

Hayden took a step back and nearly stepped on Lady.

"Watch out there," he said calmly. She needed a calm and steady hand to guide her. He took a knee next to her. Her eyes were weary as they searched him to see if she was in trouble. "You're okay."

Next stop was the kitchen. He moved into the room and walked straight over to the door to let her out. She stopped off at the water bowl for a drink before heading outside, and he grabbed a treat from the bag on the counter. He went out with her, figuring she needed to know he wasn't sticking her out there for the rest of the day.

She kept an eye on him and she seemed genuinely puzzled by his presence. It didn't stop her from doing her business.

"Treat?" he said after she was done, and she trotted over to him. He gave it over instantly. "Good girl."

Back in the house, he moved swiftly to make coffee. He glanced out the window as he waited for his cup to fill, thinking he'd never enjoyed his back porch as much as he had last night. The memory put a smile on his face. A real smile.

He reached for the necklace before realizing he'd forgotten to put it on.

With a muttered curse, he hightailed it to his bedroom. His heart pounded against his ribcage, worried that he'd misplaced it. He didn't remember taking it off last night. *Jesus.*

Lady was right on his heels as he darted across the room and to the nightstand where he always took it off at night.

It was there. Right where he left it. Safe.

Hayden blew out a sharp breath and then sat on the edge of the bed for a minute to give his heart rate a chance to calm down. He took the necklace in his hands, tossing it from one to the other. He ran his finger along the gold band, reading the inscription one more time. *Evermore.*

With a sharp sigh, he placed the necklace around his neck, pushed off the bed, and returned to the kitchen. His cup was full of dark roast, aka, manna from heaven.

He leaned a hip against the counter and took his first sip. Lady stood next to him. It looked like he'd picked up a new sidekick.

A couple of sips in, and Mika joined him in the kitchen.

"Morning," he said before going to work fixing her cup of coffee. "You're up early."

"I'd say good morning back but it still feels like last night." She stretched her arms out and he tried not to notice the cotton material of the bathrobe pulling taut across full breasts.

Hayden cleared his throat before handing over a cup of fresh brew.

"I can't remember the last time I slept so well." Her gaze dipped down to his chest, bare except for the necklace. It was the piece of jewelry that caught her attention and an unreadable look crossed her features before she turned away and walked over to the barstool tucked into the kitchen island.

When she looked up at him, the warmth he'd felt last night was gone.

It was probably for the best. He couldn't reconcile falling for someone else when he still loved LeAnne.

"How'd Lady sleep?" she asked.

"Good, but I think we gave her the wrong name." He walked around the granite island and claimed the seat near Mika's with the dog on his heels.

"Oh yeah?" Mika's forehead creased with concern. "What should we call her?"

"Shadow," he teased. "That's exactly what she's been since I brought her home."

Mika laughed despite the amusement not reaching her eyes. She was thinking about the ring. He could tell because she kept glancing down at it.

A knock at the door caused Mika to jump.

"It's probably one of my brothers or cousins," he said, setting down his coffee and heading toward the front door.

He opened it to find Coby standing on the front porch.

"Everything okay?" he asked, half scared someone else had announced they were leaving the ranch.

"Hunky-dory," Coby said. "Mind if I come in for a sec?"

"Not at all. I have company, though."

Coby's jaw nearly hit the floor. "I can come back at a... uh...later time."

"No need. Come on in." The stunned look on his brother's face was priceless. Hayden was amused.

"Are you sure?" he asked.

"Do I look like I'm uncertain?" Hayden took a dramatic step back. The cold breeze reminded him that he wasn't wearing a shirt. "Get your behind in here before I freeze."

Coby took a careful step inside like he was afraid he'd trigger a landmine.

"It's okay, man," Hayden reassured.

Coby surveyed the area, his gaze landing on Hayden's shadow.

"Who is this?" Coby took a knee.

Lady took a step behind Hayden, practically hiding behind his leg.

"She's a work in progress," Hayden said. "But she'll get there."

"I know she will." Coby stood. "Are you going to offer me a cup of coffee or what?"

"Yeah. Of course. You know where everything is." Hayden led the way with Lady on his heels. He stopped at the granite island and turned around. "This is Mika, a friend of mine."

"It's a pleasure to meet you," Coby said to her. "I'm Hayden's brother."

"The family resemblance is strong," she said. "Pleased to meet you, by the way."

"How do you guys know each other?" Coby asked as Hayden got to work on making a cup of coffee. Lady wasn't more than a half step behind.

"I work for animal control. We met through my job," she said.

"That's cool." Coby rocked his head. He was trying to play it cool, but his brother knew Hayden never had sleepovers. "Hawk asked me to pass along a message that her," he turned to face Mika, "sorry, that your car was towed into the garage first thing this morning. They'll send over an estimate ASAP."

"Thank you. That reminds me. I need to report the accident to my insurance company." She retrieved her cell and then motioned toward the stairs. "They have a twenty-four-hour hotline."

"Take your time," Coby said quickly. A little too quickly.

"Here you go, man. Try not to give me away. Okay?" Hayden handed over a cup of fresh brew.

"Sorry. You caught me off guard with this one," he said in a whisper. "I wasn't trying to blow it for you."

"Good. Because I like her a lot."

For the second time that morning, Coby's jaw nearly smacked the wood floor.

"That's good." His brother regained his composure and took a sip of coffee. He locked onto the necklace. "If you like her and you think there's a chance you might score a second date, you might not want to wear a wedding band around your neck."

Hayden issued a sharp sigh. "It just feels like a betrayal. You know?"

"You aren't doing anything wrong by living your life and part of that is dating or getting serious in a relationship," Coby said.

"I've dated," he countered and then realized what he'd done. He put his hand up as if to say *my bad.*

Normally, when his brother started into that song and dance, Hayden closed up and stopped listening. "I hear you, man. I just don't know how to turn it off. I've felt this way for so long. I can only get so far with someone and then I think about LeAnne and shut down."

"I'm guessing this one is special?" He nodded toward the hallway where she'd disappeared.

"Yes, but it's complicated. She doesn't want a relationship any more than I do," he admitted.

"I wouldn't be so sure about that," Coby said. He took a sip of his coffee.

Hayden glanced down at the necklace. "I need to throw on a shirt."

"Yes, you do. I'm not impressed, by the way." Coby flexed. "These right here are real muscles."

The teasing worked because Hayden laughed.

MIKA THREW on her clothes from yesterday after making the call to her insurance company and tucked the cell in her jacket pocket. She ran a brush through her hair and threw on a little lipstick before heading back down to the kitchen.

Coby was standing there alone, sipping a cup of coffee with his hip against the counter. The family resemblance was remarkable, but in her opinion, Hayden was by far the better-looking brother. Funny, because Coby could be on a billboard next to his brother. Hayden had charisma she found irresistible.

"Where's—"

"Hayden's getting dressed," Coby supplied with a smile. He hadn't seen her come into the room and yet he didn't seem the least bit surprised.

"Did Hayden tell me all of his brothers and cousins work at the ranch?" she asked.

"All but two, and that's a recent development," he said. "They're going into the taco business."

"Tacos?"

"Nothing like ranching, that's for sure." He nodded casually but there was nothing casual about his tone. He didn't approve or maybe he just hated the family breaking up.

"They must be incredible at making tacos for them to leave the family business." She reclaimed her coffee cup. "This is seriously the best coffee I've had in my life. And that machine makes it in, like, two seconds."

"Truth be told, I stop by here a lot in the mornings just for a cup. I always make up another excuse but this stuff is pure gold." He smiled and a dimple peeked out. Again, great looking guy for someone. She was ruined by Hayden.

"If I lived closer, I might do the same thing," she said.

Coby's gaze moved to the wedding photo on the table behind the couch. "That was a long time ago, but he still has the scars."

Was he preparing her for Hayden to push her away? The thought stung more than it should considering she had so many limitations on her life, trying to start anything up now would be silly. An annoying voice in the back of her head tried to say Hayden might be exactly what she needed to get through the coming weeks and months.

The worst part about her mother's situation was that there wasn't going to be a big prize at the end. After caring for her mother twenty-four-seven, which was the direction they were heading, she would lose the person she cared most about in the world.

"It's understandable," she said, referring to Hayden's situation. "I mean getting married so young and then losing the person he loved most in the world..."

"He told you that?" Coby sounded more than surprised. He sounded shocked.

"Yes. Last night."

"Do you mind if I ask how long the two of you have known each other?" Coby glanced at the hallway that led to the master suite. The pensive look in his eyes said he didn't want his brother to walk in on this conversation.

"Honestly? We met yesterday morning. But I can say that it feels like we've known each other a lot longer," she quickly defended because she heard how that sounded. Friends after twenty-four hours? Like, close friends. The kind who slept over each other's houses. Under normal circumstances, she would be shocked too. Except being with Hayden felt like the most natural thing in the world.

"I can see that," he said, easing some of her fears. "I'm just surprised he mentioned her. He doesn't even talk to us about the past."

The admission caught her off guard. Hayden was close to his family. She figured they talked just about everything.

"So, he told you they got married and then she got sick?"

She shook her head. "He didn't say what happened."

"My brother is going to walk into this room in a few seconds, maybe a minute. He'd probably kill me if he knew what I was about to say, but someone should," he started. "Him and LeAnne were best friends."

"He mentioned it."

"They were kids who never should have gotten married. But she..." He flashed eyes at her. "She got a rare kind of bone cancer. It was terminal. She was eighteen, going on nineteen when the news came."

Mika brought her hand up to her heart as she felt it ache for Hayden and the young woman who must've realized she would never grow up or grow old. "That's so tragic."

"It was an aggressive form of cancer, so she came home to live out whatever time she had left. She showed up at the ranch and I overheard her crying, telling my brother all of the firsts she'd never have and how her father would never get to walk his daughter down the aisle. So, he got down on one knee right then and there, and proposed marriage."

Mika sniffed away the tears welling in her eyes. She ducked her chin to her chest, trying to hide the emotions building like a tsunami.

"Later, I tried to talk him out of it but there was no use. My brother can be a mule when he wants to be and he decided to dig his heels in that day," he admitted. "God himself could've come down from the mountain to talk my brother out of the marriage and I doubt Hayden would have listened to a word."

"That's about the kindest thing I've ever heard." She couldn't fathom a greater act than for Hayden to sacrifice so much of his young self for someone else's happiness. She also couldn't compete with it but that didn't mean the two of them couldn't be friends.

The floorboard creaked in the hallway.

Coby gave her a look that she read as begging for her confidence. She gave a slight nod of understanding before changing the topic as Hayden walked in.

"Good news," she started, stalling so she could think of

what she was going to say next. "Insurance is going to come through. They'll send an adjuster later this morning."

Seeing Hayden through this new lens made her heart ache for him. For the loss he'd suffered. For the sacrifice he'd made.

She was falling even harder for this guy.

13

"I was just on my way out." Coby held up his empty coffee mug. "Thank you for this."

"Thank you for the update." Hayden looked from his brother to Mika. The air in the room had shifted. He hoped the two of them were getting to know each other a little bit while he was gone. For reasons he didn't want to examine, he wanted these two people to get along.

"No problem. I'll let the others know you're taking a couple of days off," Coby said.

"I think I said I was taking the morning off," Hayden corrected.

"Not anymore, you aren't. Besides, when was the last time you took a whole day off?" Coby started backing out of the room. "See. You can't remember and neither can I."

"I guess it's settled then."

Coby looked to Mika. "Like I said before. It's a pleasure to meet you and I hope I'm not out of line in saying that it would be nice to see you around again."

"I'd like that a lot actually," she responded.

Hayden cocked at eyebrow. He shifted his gaze from

Mika to his brother. "Remind me to ask what the two of you talked about when I was out of the room. I have a feeling I was being plotted against."

"Think what you want, brother," Coby said. Then, he winked at Mika. "But we kind of made a pact not to let you in on our little secret."

"Oh, now you're both in trouble," he teased. It was a much-needed break from the heavy thoughts he'd had earlier about LeAnne.

"That's pretty much my cue to get the heck out of here." Coby saluted Mika. "Good luck with this guy."

"Thanks. I have a feeling I'll need it," she quipped.

"Teaming up on me now, huh?" Hayden said. "I see where this is heading."

Coby ducked out the door and Mika laughed out loud.

"Sorry. Your brother cracked me up. I haven't laughed this much in a really long time," she admitted.

A stab of jealousy cut through him. He wanted to be the one to put that smile on her face.

He fixed himself a second cup of coffee and heated up a container marked, 'breakfast.'

It didn't take long for the smell of biscuits and gravy to fill the place. And bacon. He fixed two plates and set them on the table.

"Do I smell bacon?" Mika asked.

He pinched off a small piece for Lady, who took it gently from his hand after finishing off her own bowl of food.

"Sit down and eat. I'll be right back." He headed out the back door with Lady on his heels. A second later, Mika came bounding out the back door too. She shivered against the cold front that had moved in overnight. "What are you doing out here?"

"I want to be part of this." She walked up to him and

grabbed onto his arm, nestling herself against him for warmth.

"Your food will get cold," he warned.

"So will yours." She shrugged. "We'll reheat our plates if need be."

Well, didn't that sum it all up. He chuckled.

"We'll reheat," he repeated.

They stood there while Lady finished her business. Lady walked over to them and laid down. They coaxed her up and got her to follow them back inside. Hayden gave her a treat after closing the door behind her. "Good girl."

"She is a good girl," Mika said, scratching Lady behind the ears. "And she seems to have taken to you after all."

"I think you're onto something about her not trusting males in general, though," he said. "We can keep working on it."

"I should probably think about heading home." Mika changed the subject. Her ringtone sounded, and she immediately pulled her cell from her pocket and checked the screen. "It's my boss."

Hayden leaned against the counter, nodded, and then looked out the window.

"No, I hadn't heard," she said into the receiver. "Okay. What's his name again? Because I can always just stop by the sheriff's office on my way home." She paused for a long moment. "Out." Another pause. "No. I'm not home right now."

Hayden didn't like the sound of her being questioned about her whereabouts on her day off. He liked the part about stopping off at the sheriff's office even less. He and his family had spent far too much time around Sheriff Justice. He didn't have anything personal against her. By all accounts she was good at her job. She cared about the residents in her county. She was also the person who'd arrested his father.

"Oh, no. That's terrible," she continued. "Tell the sheriff that I'll swing by as soon as I can arrange a ride." Another beat passed. "I hit a deer last night." Silence. "No, I'm okay physically. It just shook me up, so I stayed over at a friend's house last night near where the incident occurred."

He shouldn't take a hit at hearing himself referred to as a friend. Yet, that was exactly what happened, and square in the chest. At least there was a heart beating in there again. No one had made him feel much of anything other than disappointment in far too long. Mika was special. Could he trust his instincts? A voice in the back of his head reminded him those instincts hadn't let him down so far. More than not, those instincts were spot on.

"I'll keep you posted," she said before ending the call. She held the cell in her hand for a long moment, staring. He took it as a sign that she needed a minute or two to regroup. It was obvious the news she'd received wasn't good.

Hayden fixed a second cup of coffee for her and set it down where she'd been sitting at the island. He turned his attention to Lady, who had positioned herself next to him. The treat bag was within reach, so he gave her a small bacon-flavored nibble.

Mika walked over to them and dropped down in front of Lady. She sat cross-legged and hugged the dog. "Mrs. Lynn, the neighbor who was feeding her was killed yesterday within an hour of me leaving. It happened some time before you took me to my service vehicle."

"Does law enforcement know the circumstances?" From the charity work his family was involved in, he knew most women were harmed by the person who had sworn to love and protect them. A fight that went too far. An affair.

Someone who fell out of love before the other was ready to let go. It sent his blood boiling to think about it. And yet, in this case, he worried the cause was even more sinister.

"No. Her husband was at work, so it couldn't have been him. His alibi is rock solid because people were around him all day. I saw her after he left for work and she looked fine. Paranoid, but in one piece."

Did that mean what he thought?

She nodded slightly, as though she could read his thoughts. She'd been cut into pieces?

"Any ideas who might have done such a horrific thing?" he asked.

"She'd been sneaking the neighbor's dog, Lady, food. And she didn't trust the man who lived there one iota. She seemed scared of him," she said. "As far as her husband knew, she wasn't in a fight with anyone." Mika paused. "She seemed like a caring soul. I mean, this girl wouldn't be alive if not for her."

Hayden issued a sharp sigh before taking a knee beside Mika and Lady. "I will forever be in her debt for her acts of kindness."

"There's more." Mika hesitated before saying the next part. "The suspect called my boss making all kinds of threats if his dog wasn't returned by the time he got home tonight."

"Over my dead body will this sweet girl leave my side."

THERE WAS no hesitation in Hayden's voice. His compassion for animals was one of the many reasons she was falling in love with him. *Love?*

Yes. There was no denying the fact she was falling hard

for Hayden McGannon. He was everything she could want in an equal partner. Kind. Considerate. Compassionate. Hard working. Fair. Generous beyond measure. Lover of all things animals. Texan through and through. Chivalrous. He lived by a code of honor. And on top of that, the man was so scorching hot she could fry an egg anywhere off his body. So, yeah, she was falling in love with him.

A relationship was something altogether different. They took time. She'd never believed in love at first sight before. Hayden was changing her mind. Because what she felt for him was something far deeper than lust or appreciation for all the things that made him beautiful. And he was beautiful inside and out.

Right now, all she wanted to focus on was the case. Because the kind neighbor had been murdered and now Mika's accident didn't feel so random. She gasped suddenly as a thought struck her. "Do you think it's possible he caused the deer to run out in front of me yesterday? I had the creepy feeling of being watched so much of the time yesterday." And then something else dawned on her. "And my jacket wasn't in the spot I normally put it."

"What jacket?" Hayden really perked up with the last bit of news.

"In my home." She flashed eyes at him. "Do you think it's possible he was inside my house?"

"Does anyone know of his whereabouts yesterday?" he asked.

She shook her head. "Not that I know of."

"So, basically, he could have been in the trailer watching everything go down?"

"That's right." A shiver rocked her body at the thought. It was highly possible. "Why wouldn't he come out and try to stop me then?"

"Witnesses," he said without missing a beat.

"Would he really be that obvious? I mean, he threatens me and my boss. He kills his neighbor after she intervenes and is seen with me. He makes an attempt on my life." Could it all be that simple?

"The evidence doesn't lie. It usually leads straight to the guilty party," he pointed out. "That being said, I agree this is coming together too easy. This guy is a hothead if he's making threats, though. And dismembering someone is a very angry way to kill them. He might have snapped off in the heat of the moment. Maybe he was unable to control his rage."

What Hayden said made perfect sense, and it scared her even more. "His name is out there, then."

"Meaning?" He cocked a brow.

"He has nothing to lose." A man who had nothing to lose wasn't a good person to have targeting her.

"Then, I don't want you out of my sight either." He brought his hand up, and then brushed the backs of his fingers against her cheek. "You've become too important to me."

Even though she was starting to get a sense the feelings between them were mutual, his past would always stop him, and her future would be all absorbing. *Shame*, she thought. What they had could have been special.

"I feel the same way, but we have to be realistic." She nodded toward his necklace and his hand came up as if protecting it. The move was instinctual, and it seemed to take him a second to catch himself mid-reach.

Slowly, he nodded.

"At least let me stay with you until they catch this creep," he said.

"If you're offering a ride to the sheriff's office, I'll take it."

She wouldn't turn down the company or the sense of protection. "Plus, any additional time I get with this girl is a bonus."

"I'll pack dinner for her in case we're out late." He moved with athletic grace while she sat on the floor with Lady.

Hayden loaded a backpack with supplies. He retrieved a red collar that had sparkly jewels on it. "A new lease on life."

"Where did you get all this stuff?"

"Derek set me up. He usually keeps a few supplies on hand for just such occasions." He started to put the collar on Lady but quickly stopped when her ears shot back, and her shackles raised. Not a good sign and Hayden seemed to know it. "You know what? We'll try it without."

"I'm wondering if she thinks the sparkle on that is like the chain she had on," Mika pointed out.

"Could be. She definitely doesn't want anything around her neck. It's a risk to take her with us without a leash, but one I'm willing to take if it helps her relax."

"She's been your shadow since we got here. I'm hoping that doesn't change because we move locations." Lady had been nothing but dedicated to Hayden after getting over the initial hump of fear.

"This should help." He grabbed the treat bag and tucked it inside the backpack.

The trio headed out after another quick sip of coffee. Lady took up basically the entire backseat. She immediately sprawled out on the blankets that he'd left there from yesterday.

"We can fix you up with a vehicle for a few days until you figure out what to do with insurance," Hayden offered.

"The agent said all I have to do is swing by and pick one up at the dealership near my home. They'd have all the paperwork ready to sign," she said. "Thank you for the offer, though."

Someone having her back for a change was something she could get used to. Other than her mother, and, honestly, she'd done her best, no one had come close. To be fair, Mika had always been independent natured and was never one to ask for help. Most took it to mean she never needed help or a cushion to soften the blows life handed out. It was so not true. Strong people needed support as much as anyone.

The drive to the sheriff's office took them past the spot of the crash.

"What are the odds someone could frighten a deer just at the moment I drove on this road?" she asked as they passed by the scene.

"You know, I've thought about that a lot since the phone call with your boss," he started. "At your home, you believed someone could have been inside when you were at work. Right?"

"Yes."

"But there were no obvious signs of break-in?"

"None that I saw. I double-checked every door and window. I probably don't have to tell you this, but I don't live in the sort of town where people routinely lock their doors," she admitted. "I started recently after receiving a few threats but that's the only reason."

"And what did you find when you checked everything?"

"The window to my laundry room was unlocked," she said.

"Someone could have slipped in and out without being detected."

"Yes." An icy chill raced down her spine at the thought someone could have been inside her house.

"Have you ever thought about installing an alarm system?" he asked.

"Not until now." Fear creeped back in, and all this should terrify her, but having him by her side was making it bearable.

14

"Come in, please." The sheriff motioned for them to take a seat in the chairs opposite her desk. She thanked her administrative assistant. "Do you mind closing the door when you leave?"

The admin nodded and then exited quietly.

"My name is Laney Justice. You can call me Laney," she said, moving around the desk and offering a firm handshake to where Mika stood next to Hayden.

"I'm Mika Taylor. Pleased to meet you."

"Hayden, it's good to see you." The familiarity shouldn't bother Mika in the least. And yet, the sheriff was beautiful. She wasn't wearing a ring. And why wouldn't Hayden be attracted to her?

Lady came in on Hayden's heels. The sheriff didn't give her a second glance. That was another benefit of small towns. No one was shocked when a dog showed up along-side a person. For the most part, people were free to live how they saw fit as long as it wasn't hurting another person or living thing. The same mindset attracted people who were territorial over what they viewed as their possessions, making her job tricky at times. Especially animal seizures. Those generally didn't go over well and the job could be considered dangerous.

Would Mika have to rethink her career now that she was basically going to be her mother's sole support? Mika's sister was turning out to be a dud, even for an occasional break.

It was good to know whether or not her sister could be counted on, though. Mika needed to make a few adjustments in her plans to care for her mother and realize that Mel wasn't going to be able to contribute much.

"Can you tell me in your own words exactly what happened yesterday morning?" Laney asked.

Mika relayed every detail she could think of, providing the events in sequence. Laney turned to Hayden next and asked for his side, which he gave in detail.

"The crime against Mrs. Lynn was violent, appearing to be an act of rage," he pointed out.

"I wouldn't disagree with that assessment," Laney said, providing confirmation they were on the right track.

"Do we know who the tenant is?" Mika asked.

Laney compressed her lips and nodded. "His name is Oliver Gaither and he's from Austin. Or, at least, that's the alias he gave in order to rent the trailer."

Mika must've looked confused.

"I did a little digging into Oliver Gaither's background. He died last year," Laney supplied.

"Murdered or natural causes?" Mika asked.

"Suspicious circumstances." Laney gave her a look.

"So, this guy has possibly killed before," Mika stated.

Hayden reached for her hand and held it in his lap. If Laney was thrown off by the gesture, she didn't show it. To an outsider, it could look like a show of support, nothing more than a kind act.

For Mika, it caused her heart to race and electricity to pulse through her. She would probably regret not sleeping with Hayden last night for the rest of her life. One night of wild abandon and the best sex of her life would...

Never mind. Because the only way to finish that sentence was...break her heart even more when she had to walk away.

No use beating that dead horse.

"Do you have any idea who this guy might actually be?" Hayden's question broke through her momentary revelry.

"Not yet. I was able to secure a warrant and I went in first thing this morning with a pair of my deputies. We figured the guy was a flight risk and we were right. He took off before we got there. Nothing in the trailer identified him on the spot. However, we collected hair samples and a couple pieces of dirty clothing that had been left behind in the laundry room. As far as fingerprints went, the place looked clean," she said.

"Not the actions of an innocent person," Hayden said.

"Afraid not." Laney clasped her hands and placed them on top of her desk.

"So, the landlord didn't run credit on the tenant before accepting him?" Mika figured the road was a dead end but it was worth a try.

"The guy paid it all in cash. Security deposit and all. Said he worked construction and a divorce took a hit to his credit. Asked if cash was acceptable, and I don't know a landlord in the world who would turn down an offer like that," Laney supplied.

"Didn't the offer cause any alarm bells to sound?" Mika couldn't believe anyone would fall for that.

"Apparently not. When I interviewed the landlord, I got

the impression the only color he cared about was green," she said.

"What about complaints on the dog?" Hayden asked. "There had to be some, right?"

"Several. The landlord received the notices and protected his cash cow tenant." Laney looked to be biting her tongue as to what her personal opinion of someone who would do that was.

"What about a description? Maybe if I knew what the suspect looked like, I could help with where I've seen him before," Mika asked.

"This is where it gets trickier. Otis James has never actually met him. Said he was moving through town on a job and would drop his rent plus deposit in Otis's mailbox. Asked the landlord to drop a key under the mat after he received payment."

"So what you're telling me is this guy is a ghost," Mika said.

"I'm afraid that's all we have on him," Laney agreed. "Mrs. Lynn's husband said they never actually saw the guy. Not good enough to give a description. The note left behind at the scene of the murder trying to implicate her husband didn't make any sense."

"He must've written it on the fly," Mika said. Domestic violence usually was the culprit in situations like these. She'd been around enough law enforcement to know how much they dreaded answering those types of calls. They were the most unpredictable and the most heated.

"DNA testing will take time," Laney warned. "I wish I had more answers for you. I'm afraid that I'm going to have to tell you to keep your eyes open."

Mika didn't think this was the right time to point out the

man could walk right by her on the street and she wouldn't know the difference.

HAYDEN HAD no plans to let Mika out of his sight.

"I'll keep you posted on anything we find out about him. My office is taking his threats seriously." Laney motioned in the direction of Lady, who was lying down underneath Hayden's chair. She was curled in a ball and he realized she'd positioned herself so that part of her was touching his leg. "I'm guessing this is the animal in question."

"Yes, and she belongs to me now," Hayden didn't hesitate to defend his claim on her, nor would he. He was ready to go to battle with anyone and everyone over this sweet dog. She deserved nothing less.

"Good. I can't think of a better home for her," Laney said before shifting her gaze to Mika. "Based on the threat, this guy has zeroed in on you."

"I've been threatened before. I can handle it." The reassurance didn't sit well with Hayden. Mainly because they didn't even have a name of who they were dealing with, let alone a description. The man killed someone in an incredibly personal and brutal way. They had no idea what his true identity was. All of which left him with an unsettled feeling the size of Houston.

Not to mention the fact that he could stick around for a day or two. But he would need to get back to his work on the ranch. Mika had a life to live. She only had a few days off to get ready for her mother before she'd be back on the job and her mother would return from Colorado.

Complicated didn't begin to describe the situation she'd

be under if they didn't find this jerk-off. Not to mention the fact they were basically searching for a ghost.

"Someone in town has to have seen this guy. A delivery driver. A postal worker. *Someone*," Hayden said.

"I'll be interviewing everyone. My deputies are already canvassing the neighbors," Laney offered.

With the houses spread apart, and people valuing their privacy in these parts, getting a description might be difficult. If the guy traveled at night, even worse. He had to have some way to make money, didn't he? Stocks? Online gambling? With computers and the internet, working from home had become easy as pie. Hayden figured someone could hide out indefinitely between meal deliveries and the internet.

Since there wasn't much more they were going to get out of Sheriff Justice, he pushed up to standing. He was pleased when Lady followed suit. He reached into the backpack and fed her a treat, which she took from his hand.

"Please call me personally if there's anything else you remember, Mika," Laney said with a gentle smile.

"Will do, Laney."

"We can see ourselves out," Hayden said to the sheriff.

Mika stared out the door first. He touched her elbow. "Will you wait in the lobby for me?"

"Of course." The look she gave him, however subtle, said he was going to have to explain once he joined her. And he would.

Once she started down the hallway, he folded his arms across his chest. "What about Donny McGannon? Is there anything new in the case that I need to be made aware of?"

"Your uncle's memory creates even more suspicion. The only thing you should know is that I plan to release him," she said matter-of-factly.

"Why would you do that?" he asked.

"He made bail."

"How?" Hayden didn't bother to hide his shock.

"You should talk to your uncle. He's the one who posted bail."

"Is that right?" He asked the question, but she seemed to realize it was rhetorical. And out of shock. He looked at her and she seemed just as surprised by it as he was.

She shrugged. "What can I say? Family bonds run strong."

"When do you plan to release him?" Hayden needed to get word to the rest of his family. This was definitely going to cause a wrinkle in any attempt for him, his brothers, and cousins to get on better footing. In fact, it felt like he'd just had the rug pulled out from underneath him.

"Could be as early as tomorrow. I'm waiting on word from Judge Andress," she admitted.

"Is anyone else in my family aware aside from my uncle?"

She shook her head.

"I'll let my brothers know." He also needed to call his cousin Levi. He was technically the oldest in the family and would probably want to have a meeting to discuss what their next steps should be. Surely, no one wanted Donny McGannon back on ranch property. Not even their uncle must want that. "Thank you for the information."

"You bet."

Hayden showed himself out with Lady on his heels. Head down, she kept a close distance to him.

Mika was seated in the secure area, waiting for him. She was perched on the edge of her seat, wringing her hands together. "Everything okay?"

He must've had a look on his face. "Got some interesting information."

She stood up and he linked their fingers.

"I'll tell you about it in the truck," he said, leading her out the door. The local hospital and the sheriff's office were two places he wouldn't mind never seeing the inside of again as long as he lived.

Scanning the parking lot for any signs of threat, he walked Mika to the passenger side of the truck. Lady hopped in after he gave her a drink of water by grabbing a bottled water and then pouring it in his hand, making a makeshift bowl.

The dog lapped up the water before hopping into the backseat and making herself comfortable. Once Mika was inside, he surveyed the area again before reclaiming the driver's seat.

"I need your address," he said. She gave it over and he programmed it into GPS. When she leaned over to check it, he did what he'd been wanting to do all morning. Kissed her.

She tasted like a mix of dark roast and peppermint toothpaste. He never thought he'd like those two flavors mixed together. On her, he could get used to it. In fact, he could learn to love it. And now every time he had a cup of coffee immediately after brushing his teeth, he would think about her.

He pulled back and started the engine, thinking that she was right to point out the necklace to him earlier. It would be impossible to move on from LeAnne when he kept reminders of her everywhere.

Did he want to move on?

The question caught him off guard as he exited the parking lot. There was no immediate answer that came to mind. All he knew for certain was that he could see a future with Mika, and that was foreign to him.

Tabling the thought for now, he filled her in on his family situation.

"How do you feel about your father's release?" she asked.

"I can't avoid him forever," he admitted. "It was a helluva lot easier to do when he was in jail, though."

"Blood ties run strong," she said.

He couldn't agree more. "It has to be the only reason my uncle would post bail—bail I didn't even know was an option."

"Maybe your uncle leaned on the judge a little bit? Your family has a lot of connections. It wouldn't be outside the realm of possibility for your uncle to use some of his influence to have his brother released."

"I can't even imagine why he would do that for the man who quite possibly tried to kill him. At the very least, my father tried to conspire against Uncle Clive."

"Your uncle sounds like an extraordinary person," she said.

She was dead on. His father was another case altogether.

15

Mika watched her street with weary eyes now that she knew someone might be stalking her. It was the logical explanation for the accident. The stalker could have followed her home. He could have been waiting for the right opportunity to strike. Making her death look like an accident would stop any investigation.

But why didn't the person come out of the woods? She could reason the timing of the deer. But why not come out of the woods and finish the job?

The answer came to her in a flash of inspiration that came with an icy chill. "I was on the phone with you."

"Come again?" Hayden had been lost in his own thoughts after the revelation about his father.

"I could have shouted out his description," she reasoned. "The eyes I felt on me last night. It could have been him. He might have seen an opportunity to spook a deer into my path and then he planned to finish me off. Ever since this happened, I couldn't understand why he didn't just go ahead and do it last night."

"We were on the phone and you could have shouted out

who he was or what he looked like." Hayden rocked his head.

"Yes."

He parked in the cul-de-sac in front of her house.

"Makes sense," he said.

"He may have figured out my schedule by being inside my house." Another one of those icy shivers raced down her back at the thought a stranger—a killer!—had so easily slipped inside her home. She would definitely call about getting an alarm installed once this was all over. It was crazy that she even needed one, but not facing reality never made it disappear. She had a dangerous job. The other recent threats against her made her realize anyone could come after her at almost any time. Would she be prepared?

In the past, she would have said a resounding *yes*. Now that she was going to be responsible for more than just herself, she wasn't so certain. Much of her current job was losing its appeal. She was already having one life crisis. A job change was time intensive, and change was stressful. She was pretty certain she'd read an article recently about job changes ranking right up there with moving as one of life's biggest stressors.

This didn't seem like the time to uproot her job despite realizing the shine had worn off recently. Actually, when she really thought about it, the long hours had been getting to her since before her mother's condition.

All work and no social life was wearing thin, but she couldn't see herself in a job that didn't involve caring for animals. Her placements were right up there with some of her proudest accomplishments.

"Does anything look out of the ordinary?" he asked, checking out her street.

"No. There aren't any cars I don't recognize. Looks like

several of my neighbors are home today." She surveyed her house, thinking how violated she felt that some creep had been walking around in there while she was none the wiser. Anger rippled through her because she refused to let him—whoever 'he' was—turn her into a victim. The vulnerability she felt made her want to scream and get to the gym for a few rounds with a punching bag.

"Let's head inside." He hopped out of the vehicle and was at her side in a beat. He opened the door as she grabbed the handle. Lady hopped out and then did her business on the lawn. The water seemed to have made its way through her. The fact she was doing so well in such a short time was a rare bright spot in this situation. Between Lady and meeting Hayden, the situation wasn't all grim. She'd take whatever silver lining she could grab onto.

Perspective was important. Otherwise, it would be easy to let herself be consumed with fear. The guy who was stalking her was a coldblooded killer.

Glancing around, she shouldered her purse and exited the truck. The walk to her front door had never felt so long.

"Would it be possible for you to give me a ride to the dealership later, to get my rental?" she asked.

"I'll take you anywhere you want." He followed her inside her house and then stopped at the door. He scanned the living room before making his way to the kitchen to check the back door. There were no signs of forced entry. The doors were still locked. And so was the laundry room because he checked there next. When they were back in the living room, he continued, "My only request is that you let me stick around for a day or two. Just until law enforcement gets this whole scenario under control."

"You won't get any arguments out of me." Granted, it was going to be that much more difficult to say goodbye when this was over. Walking away from Hayden was going to be the hardest thing she'd ever done. That, she was certain.

"Does that mean you'll let us stay?" The twinkle in his eyes wasn't helping her keep a grip on her emotions. Falling for Hayden any further would be a mistake.

He took a step toward her and her heart free fell. *Falling for Hayden would be a big mistake.* She repeated the words in her mind, hoping they would stick this time

He brought his hands up to cup her face. *Falling for Hayden would be a big mistake.* This was becoming her mantra at this point.

And then he kissed her. His mouth moved against hers, slow and tender. So much so, it robbed her breath. The butterflies in her chest took flight as she brought her hands up to his shoulders, digging her fingers in to anchor herself. Her pulse raced and her breath quickened.

When they finally broke apart, she needed a minute to catch her breath. He did too and a little piece of her was thrilled she was having the same effect on him that he was having on her.

Something was bugging her about the crime scene picture that Laney had shown them. Something other than the brutality of the crime and the blood that had seemed like it was everywhere. Her heart went out to Mr. Lynn. She couldn't imagine the horror of walking in the door from work and finding a loved one had been murdered. The violation of it happening in their home was even worse.

Lady moved from Hayden's side. Nose to the ground, she seemed to pick up on a scent. She went straight to the stairs as Hayden and Mika followed. Next, Lady moved from the office to the master bedroom. She immediately went to the closet. Mika registered that the dog skipped over the hall

bath. However, she'd gone all the way inside the office and
around to the back of Mika's desk.

Was she tracking the movements of a recent strange
scent? The scent of her previous owner?

Mika rubbed her arms to stave off the sudden chill.

In the bedroom, Lady had immediately gone toward
Mika's closet but stopped short at the clothes basket.
Hold on...

Mika moved to the basket and started throwing clothes
onto the floor, searching for her favorite warmups. They
were nowhere to be found. And then it dawned on her.

"He was inside my house. I'm one hundred percent
certain of it now," she said to Hayden. He stood at the door-
way, his hands against the doorjamb.

"Did he take something?" he asked.

"Yes. My favorite warmups are missing. The other day,
my work jacket, which I one hundred percent know I left on
the back of a chair in the living room, ended up in my office.
My memory has been a little wonky lately with everything
going on in my personal life, but I never bring my jacket
upstairs. I chalked it up to losing my mind, but this is no
accident."

Then, she gasped. She knew exactly what had been
niggling away at the back of her mind after viewing the
crime scene photo. "He made her change into my clothes
before he killed her."

"Are you certain?" Hayden couldn't hide the shock in his
voice. Based on her wide eyes, she was just as much caught
off guard as she'd been by the revelation. "Never mind. I
know you are. We need to give Laney a call."

Mika was already nodding her head. "I left my phone downstairs."

He followed her, thinking he had a phone call to make as well. His was to his brothers about their father. He could put Reed and Coby on conference call mode and deliver the news to both at the same time. He'd let Reed take charge of notifying the others.

While Mika made a call to the sheriff, he attempted to get his brothers on the line. He had no idea if it was possible considering all the dead zones on the ranch. Reed answered.

"Everything okay?" The concern in Reed's voice told Hayden that Coby had most likely updated their brother on the sleepover situation.

"I'm fine," he reassured. He realized they were coming out of a place of caring, so he wouldn't allow himself to get upset about the invasion of privacy. They cared. He couldn't fault them for it. "I have some news and I'd like to get Coby on the line before I talk about it."

"Oka-a-y-y." The way his brother drew out the word said he hadn't heard about their father yet.

Hayden added their brother to the call. At least one thing was going Hayden's way today when Coby picked up on the first ring.

"Are you all right?" There was so much concern in Coby's voice that Hayden realized his brothers were most likely staying in cell range in case he needed one of them.

"I'm good. I have Reed on another line. I'm going to join up the calls. Hang on for a second. If I lose you, I'll call you right back."

"Sounds like a plan."

With a touch on his screen, the three of them were on the line together. Hayden wasn't one for staring at a screen all day, but he had to admit the devices came in handy in times like these.

"We should all be on the line," Hayden said.

"I'm here," Reed confirmed.

"Same for me," Coby chimed in.

"Good. There's no easy way to say this, so I'll just come out with it. I was at the sheriff's office today with my friend Mika. When our meeting was over, I asked the sheriff about our father."

"And?" Reed didn't miss a beat.

"She let me know that Uncle Clive posted bail for Dad. He'll be released as soon as the final paperwork comes through."

"Are you serious?" Coby didn't bother to hide his shock.

Reed was quiet. He always did like to mull something over before adding his two cents. Then came, "Uncle Clive believes Dad is innocent."

"Is that naïve, though?" Hayden asked the question that had to be on everyone's mind.

"Maybe," Reed admitted. "It's also hopeful and what family does for each other."

"True," Coby added.

"I understand that. Believe me, I do. But we're not talking about bailing someone out for making moonshine in the barn," Hayden said.

"That would be a fire hazard." Reed could be so literal.

"You know what I mean. We're talking about attempted murder here," Hayden continued. "I don't need to remind anyone who Dad is accused of trying to kill or how much he could stand to gain if something happened to Uncle Clive."

Again, the line went quite for a few seconds that dragged on.

"I've given this situation a whole lot of thought," Reed

began. "As I'm sure the two of you have. I couldn't say one way or the other if Dad is capable of trying to kill his brother. I don't have the faintest idea what our father is capable of because I don't know the man."

There were a couple of grunts of agreement.

"That's on me, though. Our father came back to work at the ranch. When he talked to me about trying to get more of the pie, he envisioned us working together. I'm not saying he went about things the right way or that what he tried to convince me was honorable in any way. He's not half the man his brother is. But if I'm going to make my own determination as to whether or not he's a greedy killer, I'm going to have to get to know him a little." Reed didn't try to talk them into going along with him. He was just stating facts as he saw them.

"It looks like you'll get your chance now that he's being released." Hayden wasn't so sure he could go there.

"I'm not sure I care about getting to know a man who had no qualms about walking away from us," Coby said after a thoughtful pause.

"Agreed," Hayden said.

"I'm not going to try to convince you otherwise. You guys have to follow your own hearts." There was no judgment in Reed's tone, just a statement of facts as he saw them.

"Will you tell Levi and the others? I have my hands full here over the next couple of days." Hayden didn't mention their absentee brothers specifically, but Reed would know he meant them as well.

"Will do." Reed's voice shifted to concern. "Everything okay in your neck of the woods?"

"I need to be out for a few days, maybe more. I'm helping a friend who is in trouble and she might need an extra set of eyes to keep her safe." He wanted to stay with Mika until the killer was caught. The last bit of news about a murderer sneaking inside her home and stealing her clothes was unsettling as all get out. This jerk had to be a real twisted creep to pull something like this.

"Do you need backup?" Reed asked.

"You'll be the first one I call if I do." Hayden meant every word. It felt good to open up and let his family in even if it was just a little bit. Baby steps, but he'd take 'em. And he had Mika to thank for this newfound feeling. She made him want to push through the pain and let others in his life. He quickly briefed them on the current situation. They needed to know, especially considering the trailer area wasn't too far off from McGannon property. It was nowhere near the residences, but still. A killer was on the loose. Word would get out soon. And he didn't want his family to be blindsided by the news.

"It goes without saying, but take whatever time you need," Reed said. "We'll keep everything covered on our end and we'll keep a vigilant watch."

"The timing isn't great considering..." He couldn't bring himself to call out his brothers.

"That's why we work as a team. We'll keep everything covered on this end. You just take care of whatever you need to on yours."

"If you need any one of us, all it takes is a phone call and we'll be headed your way." Reed's sentiment was immediately confirmed by Coby.

"Hearing you say it means the world," was all Hayden could say. He meant every word.

They exchanged goodbyes and his mind swerved back toward Mika. Who did she have to lean on when times were tough? And based on what she'd told him, clearing a killer out of the way was one thing. Her mother's condition was another. Mika was strong and persevered through adversity that would take most people down or, at the very least, make them feel sorry for themselves. There was not a hint of either in Mika. In fact, she seemed like she was gathering her strength for the long battle ahead—a battle she refused to cave underneath. Based on the conversation he'd overheard with her sister last night and what she'd shared about their father, she was going to battle with a one-man army.

Why did the thought cause Hayden's chest to hurt? Why did the idea of her bravely going it alone feel like such a gut punch?

The annoying voice chose that moment to pipe up...*because you want to be there with her, side-by-side, facing life together.*

The realization was a face slap. He tried to mentally shake it off.

16

Walking around the house shouldn't cause the tiny hairs on the back of Mika's neck to prickle. She searched for something to take her mind off the creepy thoughts rolling around in her head about a murderer being inside her home as she waited for a deputy to arrive.

The first thought that popped into her mind was how grateful she was that her mother was in Colorado instead of here.

Hayden walked into the living room after ending a call. "My brothers are now aware of what's about to go down with our father."

He walked straight over to her, dipped his head down, and pressed a kiss to her lips. There was something about Hayden, about the calmness that came over her when he was near, that made her feel like her world wouldn't implode after all.

The reality of her current situation struck like lightning. Letting her guard down, even for a second, would be a mistake.

"He was sending me a message," she said. "I can feel it."

When she looked at Hayden, she realized he'd been studying her.

"What do you think about coming to stay with me at the ranch until this whole situation blows over?" he asked. There was a storm brewing behind those gorgeous brown eyes of his.

"There's no reason for me to be home right now, considering my mother's away." Being away from this place sounded pretty good to her right now. She was still angry and creeped out by the fact the jerk was able to slip inside her home undetected. Part of her wanted to take a stand and reclaim her home. The logical part won. It reminded her that she was facing down a cold-blooded killer and needed to take every precaution possible. "Staying at the ranch for a few days to give law enforcement a chance to do their jobs sounds like a good idea to me."

The doorbell rang, causing Mika to jump.

"It's probably the deputy," she said, making a beeline for the door. She checked out the peephole to find a man in a brown deputy's uniform standing on her porch. She heard the squawk of the radio. She opened the door.

"Afternoon, Ms. Taylor."

"Come on..." Hold on a minute. She'd never met this guy. How did he know her name? She instinctively started closing the door. The deputy's voice was certain of who she was and he would only know that if he'd seen her before, which he hadn't.

The stranger wedged the toe of his boot inside to stop her from shutting him out.

A shot of adrenaline pumped through her as her pulse quickened. Hayden was making a beeline for the door as she struggled to keep it from slamming open.

A low, throaty growl ripped from Lady.

"Get over here and shut up," the man posing as a deputy commanded. He was a little too familiar with her not to be the man they were searching for.

"The sheriff is on her way," Mika said.

"Her deputy has been detained." Those words sent a cold chill racing down Mika's spine as Hayden joined her at the door. Just before he could get his hands on it, she lost the battle and the door smacked into her shoulder.

A blow so fierce knocked her back a step, straight into Hayden. She lost her balance, but he righted her. The distraction of helping her allowed the killer to step inside the door and close it behind him. Mika tried to remember where she'd last put her weapon. She came up empty. Normally, it would be in her holster upstairs in her closet. She never kept it downstairs, especially after her mother had moved in.

The thought this man had killed a deputy on his way to get her caused her heart to ache. It was then she saw the streaks of blood on the back of the shirt. But she couldn't focus on the loss right now.

Lady was going crazy behind them, growling. Her shackles were raised and her ears were back.

Hayden took a punch to the jaw so hard his head snapped back. And that's when she saw the killer pull a weapon from behind him. The knife must have been tucked in the waistband of his jeans, hidden from view when he was at the door.

Frustration nailed her at falling for his trick and opening the door. She'd handed all three of them over on a silver platter.

"Take Lady and get out of here," Hayden warned.

There was no way she was leaving him. Yes, the killer

wanted her. But he'd just kill Hayden and then find her anyway. There was no way she was running. This stopped here and now.

She watched as the tall and thick killer wrestled Hayden to the ground. Rapid fire barks were coming out of Lady at this point. The killer rolled over and fired off a punch to shut her up. Mika grabbed the dog in time and got nipped at in the process. She was fine and succeeded in stopping him from hurting Lady.

The distraction gave Hayden a chance to get in a solid uppercut. The killer's head snapped back, giving Hayden a chance to go for the long, serrated blade in Killer's hand.

Mika waited for her chance. She was afraid to go upstairs and leave them alone. Frantic, she scanned the room, realizing she could do some damage with the heavy crystal vase on the bookshelf. She ran to it, and then gripped it with both hands.

She inched closer to the fight that had turned into a wrestling match.

Blood squirted onto the floor as one of them grunted. Panic filled her chest causing her ribcage to squeeze. *No. No. No.*

Taking a risk, she moved closer to the tangle of bodies, hands, and feet. Hayden spun around, ending up on top. Blood dripped from his elbow as he struggled to take control of the knife. There was blood on his shirt too.

Panic gripped her as she saw her opportunity to strike. Without hesitating, she seized the moment. Moving in quickly, she slammed the vase into the killer's skull. For a split-second, he looked at her with the blackest eyes—eyes that would haunt her for the rest of her days. A shiver rocked her body. And then, his gaze unfocused, like he was looking inside himself and his head dropped, hitting the floor.

Hayden wasted no time spinning the guy around onto his back, removing the knife and tossing it across the room. He pinned the killer in between his powerful thighs.

His face paled. He was losing a lot of blood.

"Call for help," he said and she could tell he was holding onto consciousness by a thread.

No. No. No.

She immediately raced to her cell and called 911, keeping her gaze on Hayden the entire time.

"Nine-one-one, what's your emergency?" the operator asked as Mika put the call on speaker.

"A killer is in my house. The killer," she managed to get out. "And I need an ambulance right away."

What else could she do?

Stop the bleeding. She needed to assess Hayden's condition and stop the bleeding. Dear Lord, let her stop the bleeding.

"Ma'am, are you in a safe place?"

"No." She set the phone on the coffee table and moved to Hayden.

"You're going to be okay," he said. His lips were turning blue. "We got him."

"No. I won't ever be okay without you. Hang on for me, Hayden. Please," she begged.

The color had drained from his face—his beautiful face.

"Where are you hurt?" she asked.

"Me? I'm not." He opened his eyes and glanced down at his body, his arm. Blood pulsed from below his bicep. He muttered the same curse she was thinking. "Take my shirt."

He shrugged out of it while she helped. She knew exactly what he wanted her to do. She'd been thinking the exact same thing. Using the cotton material, she tied off his arm below the shoulder in a makeshift tourniquet.

The trick worked. The flow of blood was stemmed.

"Hold on until help arrives, Hayden."

BASED ON MIKA'S REACTION, Hayden figured he didn't look real good about then. He struggled to stay conscious as he performed a quick body check to look for more wounds. There were a couple of cuts on his torso, nothing a little antibacterial gel couldn't fix up.

His gaze flew to Lady. She stood in the corner, back against the wall, looking like she'd bite anyone who cornered her there.

"You're okay," Hayden soothed, trying to calm her as he fought against the darkness tugging at him from the inside out.

"And so are you," Mika stated, matter of fact, like there was no other option.

"Take care of her..." His energy was draining fast.

"No. I won't. Because you will. You're going to be okay and you're going to take care of this sweet girl because she's counting on you. *I'm* counting on you and you can't leave me now. I'm in love with you, Hayden. Did you hear me?"

He blinked his eyes open to see tears streaming down Mika's beautiful face.

"No. No. No. Don't you dare go anywhere, Hayden. Stay right here." Her voice became more and more distant.

He tried to focus on it. To hear the sound of her sweet voice. He *wanted* to stay with her. There was something important he wanted to tell her. He could feel the words right there on the tip of his tongue even though he couldn't seem to make his mouth move.

Mika screamed. Sirens split the air. And then everything went black.

MIKA SPRANG into action as Hayden slumped over and the killer slowly opened his eyes. She grabbed anything she could find on the coffee table. Her hand landed on a hard-back book. She slammed it into the man's face.

He grunted in pain as he pushed Hayden off him. Hayden's head smacked against the wood flooring hard.

"Help," she screamed as she scooted backward, feeling around for the knife. She could only hope the emergency dispatcher was still on the line. "Short blonde hair. Blue eyes. Runner's build with a little more muscle than expected. Six-feet-two-inches is a guess. Male. Caucasian." Shouting out his description would give authorities someone to look for if she didn't make it out alive.

Lady fired off angry-sounding barks. A warning not to get any closer.

Mika scrambled to stay out of his reach. Her fingertip grazed metal. The knife. She palmed it, scooting back until she was so close to Lady the barking reverberated inside Mika's head.

"Blackjack, cut it out. It's your master," the killer said through clenched teeth as he crawled toward them.

Mika was beside Lady now, thankful the dog hadn't bitten her yet. Lady was in danger mode and she didn't want anything to do with the man coming toward her. Mika feared Lady might listen to him. He left her alone too much. It was the only logical explanation. She'd been territorial about her yard. She would view it as her personal space. But this man? She didn't know from Adam.

As he inched towards her, Mika drew her foot up to her chest and then fired off a kick. He grabbed her foot.

Lady's barks intensified as Mika struggled to pull away from him.

"Ma'am, help is almost there," came from the speaker on the coffee table.

The man grabbed the cell and chunked it against the wall. He scrambled to get up, while pulling Mika's leg up with him.

"It's your time to die, bitch." He yanked her ankle toward the ceiling.

Lady lunged at him, clamping her teeth around his kneecap. He dropped Mika's leg and shouted in pain.

The distraction was all Mika needed to regroup. She tightened her grip around the knife handle. She reared her hand back. And then, as though on a spring, she released.

The killer bent forward to punch Lady. His fist never made it. Mika rammed the knife inside him, catching him just below the clavicle. He was lucky he'd moved or she would have hit her target—his heart.

He stumbled back a couple of steps, clearly in shock. He brought his right hand up to try to pull the knife out as the front door burst open. Laney Justice stood there. The business end of her gun aimed directly at the killer, the man who was no longer a ghost.

He wouldn't be able to hide behind a fake identity any longer.

"Hayden," was all Mika could say.

"Hands where I can see 'em," Laney commanded in the voice reserved for cops.

The killer complied as Mika cut around him, gunning

toward Hayden's side. She immediately checked his pulse. Got one. It was weak.

"Hands against the wall," Laney demanded.

He complied.

"He has a knife stuck in him just below the left clavicle," Mika informed.

"Turn around and keep your hands high," Laney instructed.

A pair of EMTs followed her inside as she arrested him. The background noise of rights being read faded as Mika pushed back so the EMTs could go to work on Hayden.

Within minutes, her home was filled with emergency workers and law enforcement. Hayden was loaded up on a gurney and then placed in the back of an ambulance.

Another set of EMTs stabilized the killer.

"Keep him alive," Mika said as she walked past. "He needs to rot in jail. Dying is too easy."

"You got it, ma'am," one of the EMTs shot back.

Mika was caught between a rock and a hard place. She wanted to follow the ambulance, but someone had to stay with Lady. Hayden would want it to be her.

"I need to notify Hayden's family of what happened," she said to Laney as the sheriff waited for her handcuffed prisoner to be either field dressed or loaded in the back of the second ambulance. "I have no idea how to reach them."

"I have their numbers," Laney offered.

"Yes. Please." Mika handed over her cell. "Do you mind putting them in. I doubt I could manage." Her hands shook as she she sat on the floor next to Lady, who'd calmed down considerably.

"Not at all." Laney took the phone and programmed in the contacts before handing it back.

"Thank you." Mika took the offering. The dog was still

visibly shaken so she forced herself to stand and then went to Hayden's treat bag. She brought Lady a treat. "Good girl."

A tear leaked out of Mika's eye as she thought about the fact this dog had just saved her life. Hayden's too. If that man had gotten to Mika, Hayden would have been finished off next. He was already weak. It wouldn't have taken much.

"I can make sure she's taken care of while you go to the hospital," Laney offered.

"No, but thank you. She's my responsibility until she can be reunited with her owner." More of those tears streaked Mika's face as she made the call no one wanted to have to make to Hayden's brothers.

17

Mika stood next to Lady in the parking lot of the county hospital. One truck roared up, followed by the second.

She recognized the first driver as Coby. The family resemblance to the second driver was strong. Reed was Hayden's older brother.

The two men hopped out of their vehicles as others arrived.

"The family is here and more are coming," Coby said as he brought Mika into a hug. "You can go inside now. I'll stay with Lady."

Mika glanced from Coby to Reed, who also urged her to go. She bent down to scratch Lady behind the ears. "If it wasn't for this girl, neither one of us would be alive."

"We'll take good care of her," Coby reassured.

Mika took in a sharp breath before kissing the dog on the forehead and handing over a bag of treats. "She loves these."

Coby took the bag and gave one to Lady. "Let us know how he's doing in there. Okay?"

"You got it." Mika took off in a half jog, half run toward the entrance to the hospital. She already knew the details. Seventh floor. Check in with the nurses.

The elevator couldn't get there fast enough. She tapped her foot on the cold tile. The ding was never more welcomed.

On the seventh floor, she stopped at the nurse's station. "Hayden McGannon's room, please."

"Are you next of kin?" the nurse asked.

A second nurse turned around. "What's your name, hon?"

"Mika Taylor."

"You go right ahead. Room 714," the older nurse over-rode the first. "He's asking for you."

"Thank you." Mika made a beeline for his room.

Nothing could prepare her for the image of strong and masculine Hayden hooked up to beeping machines. She stopped after taking one step inside.

"Hey," his voice was raspy. "Come in."

She rushed to his side and grabbed hold of his hand. "I thought I lost you."

Emotion got the best of her and tears leaked from her eyes.

"Think you can get rid of me that easy?" With some effort, he brought her hand up to his lips. "Not a chance."

"I just didn't know...you looked so..."

"All I needed was a little oxygen and to stem the bleeding. They did most of the work in the ambulance. By the time I got here, I was already doing better. Now, I'm here for the night for fluids. I suspect the doctor wants to make sure I don't get up and around." He sounded good and alert. Tired, but good.

She sighed relief.

"They got him. He's going to spend the rest of his life behind bars."

"Good."

"Lady was a hero, just like you."

He shook his head.

"You said something back in your house and I," he paused to catch his breath, "wanted to know if I imagined it."

Nothing came to mind. She'd been in too much of a panic to remember very much. "Tell me what it is and I'll let you know for sure."

"You said you loved me and couldn't lose me. Is that true?"

She nodded. "Nothing has even been truer. And I know our lives are complicated—"

"That's the thing. They don't have to be."

She must have shot him quite the look because he put a hand up and winced.

"Love isn't complicated. You either love someone and make a commitment or you don't. It's simple when you really think about it."

Was he implying what she thought he was?

"I love you, Mika."

"I love you too. But I have my moth—"

"No 'buts' about it. Your family is my family. When I say that I love you, I mean that it's forever. I've never met anyone like you. You're intelligent. You're beautiful. You're compassionate. Your heart is bigger than Texas, which I didn't even think was possible. And I want to marry you. So, if you'll have me and forgive me for not being able to get down on one knee, I'm asking you to be my wife."

Well, now the tears really were streaming. No sadness. Tears of happiness. Sweet tears of release.

"Yes, Hayden. I'll marry you. I've lived long enough to know that I'll never meet anyone who gets me in the way you do. Or who is a better match. We might not know little things about each other yet. But I'd like to spend the rest of our lives learning those nuances about each other. I love you and will never love anyone more than you."

This time, she kissed him. Long. Thorough. Sweet.

Home.

18

EPILOGUE

Coby stood on the lawn where he'd played countless baseball games growing up. He looked across the expansive lawn thinking they'd had too little to celebrate since his father had come home until recently when his brothers and cousins had met their equal partners in life.

Hell, he never thought he'd see the day when Hayden settled down again after what he'd been through. Good for him. Mika would make a beautiful bride and one heck of an addition to the family.

And then there were three, he mused. He could count on one hand how many single guys there were left in the family.

"It's just you and me, kid," Coby said to his faithful companion, Diesel. It wasn't a complaint so much as a statement of fact.

Miss Penny's smile was ear-to-ear as she stood off to one side by one of the many punchbowls with Hawk. Neither would come right out and admit they were in a relationship but it was so obvious to everyone around that's exactly what was happening.

But, hey, it was their business. If they thought they were getting one over on people with their 'secret', he wasn't going to be the one to burst their bubble. He loved and respected both of them too much for that. But everything, including the way their bodies were turned toward each other and shutting out everyone else, said they were in love.

Who would have thought? Miss Penny had sworn off men ages ago. Said she already had all the loves of her life underneath one roof. He always wondered why she'd never married but was too polite to ask about a subject that seemed off limits. If she didn't want to talk about her past, far be it from him to force the issue. Coby was a live-and-let-live type. As long as people were decent to each other and respected each other's boundaries, there was no reason for him to know or judge their choices.

A hot new country band, See-Sawer, was setting up on what used to be home plate. Their crew had set up a makeshift stage. Soon, the air would be filled with something besides all this goofy-eyed love. Don't get him wrong, he couldn't be happier for his family members who'd found 'the one.' And he'd raise a glass to each one when the time was right.

From the corner of his eye, he saw Miss Penny heading toward him. She was holding out a red Solo cup in her hands as she approached.

"Hello there," she started, thrusting the cup at him rather aggressively. Her impish smile said she was up to no good.

"What is that?" he asked, taking the forced offering.

"What?" She batted her eyelashes rather innocently.

Whatever was going on was far from innocent. "It's just a little cup of water."

"Very funny." He looked into the cup and swirled the liquid around for a few seconds.

"Go on. Drink up," she urged. Her face broke into a wide smile now. She knew full well there wasn't much he wouldn't do for her.

The running joke between some of his family members was that there must be something in the water because everyone seemed to be pairing up all of a sudden. The all of a sudden part was partially true. The relationships had happened within the span of a handful of months.

"You know I don't believe in any of that stuff," he warned. He was playing around with her and it felt good to be lighthearted for a change.

"Well then, it shouldn't bother you to finish it off," she reasoned. He couldn't argue her logic.

He bent down and kissed her on the top of her head, winked. "I'll drink it when I'm thirsty."

His answer seemed to satisfy her. She clapped her hands as the band started to play.

"You sure did a great job with the decorations, Miss Penny. I'd say you outdid yourself."

"Do you think anyone will use the dance floor?" she asked. Her eyes lit up as she saw Hawk making his way toward them.

"With music like this, how could they not?"

And just like out of a fairy tale book, Hawk held his hand out, gave a slight bow, and asked Miss Penny to dance.

"I'd be honored," she said, taking his hand. She turned to Coby with a sudden worried look. "Will you be all right over here all by yourself?"

"I'm not alone," he said quickly. "I've got Diesel."

An emotion flickered behind those all-knowing eyes of hers before she conceded with a smile.

"Let your guard down once in a while," she said. "You never know when you might realize the person you were meant to be with was standing in front of you all along."

"I'll keep that in mind," he said mostly out of respect. He didn't want her worrying about him. She'd done her part, stepping up to raise him, his brothers, and their cousins. She deserved some time for herself.

As for looking around Cattle Cove for a date, he'd been there, done that, and had long lost the T-shirt. Besides, there was too much going on in the family to worry about finding a date. And with two of his brothers ducking out of the family and several others getting married, his workload would only increase.

Besides, he was Donny's son, not Clive's. He came from the bad brother.

Speaking of dear old Dad, he was in jail instead of here with family because his release was held up. And there was a reason for that. He couldn't say it was unlike any other major family milestone his father had missed. This time, he had no choice in the matter. And there was no reason to strike up a relationship with dear old Dad now when the man might be sent away to prison for the rest of his life.

The thought struck Coby harder than he expected. He might not respect his father, but the thought of him living out the rest of his life in prison didn't sit well. Coby was human and didn't wish that on his worst enemy.

He swirled the water around in his cup a few more times. And then he dumped it onto the grass. "You need this more than I do."

Looking out onto the lawn as couples made their way onto the dance floor, a dull ache formed in Coby's chest.

What was that all about? He didn't need anyone. His life was good here on the ranch. He loved the land. He loved his family. He didn't want or need anyone.

So, why did the ache only get stronger when he looked out over the lawn?

TO CONTINUE READING Coby's story, click here.

ALSO BY BARB HAN

Texas Grit

Kidnapped at Christmas

Murder and Mistletoe

Bulletproof Christmas

For more of Barb's books, visit www.BarbHan.com.

ABOUT THE AUTHOR

Barb Han is a USA TODAY and Publisher's Weekly Best-selling Author. Reviewers have called her books "heartfelt" and "exciting."

Barb lives in Texas—her true north—with her adventurous family, a poodle mix and a spunky rescue who is often referred to as a hot mess. She is the proud owner of too many books (if there is such a thing). When not writing, she can be found exploring Manhattan, on a mountain either hiking or skiing depending on the season, or swimming in her own backyard.

Sign up for Barb's newsletter at www.BarbHan.com.